I was Hitler's cat

N.J. Dodic

Gutter Press

The publisher gratefully acknowledges the assistance of The Ontario Arts Council and The Canada Council for the Arts.

  Canada Council   Conseil des Arts
                     for the Arts   du Canada
ONTARIO ARTS COUNCIL
CONSEIL DES ARTS DE L'ONTARIO

National Library of Canada Cataloguing in Publication
Dodic, N. J., 1965-
I was Hitler's cat / N.J. Dodic.
"A Sam Hiyate book."
ISBN 1-896356-37-0
I. Title.
PS8557.O2265I5 2002   C813'.54   C2002-902066-2
PR9199.3.D528I5 2002

Published by Gutter Press, P.O. Box 600, Station Q,
Toronto, Ontario, Canada M4T 2N4
email: gutter@gutterpress.com

Represented and Distributed in Canada by
Publishers Group West Canada, 250A Carlton St.
Toronto, Ontario, Canada M5L 2L1

Design...4dT

Manufactured in Canada

The author wishes to thank Leslie Pasternack for her editorial assistance.

For Vera

Off the Streets and into the Bunker

If, as Mr. Bumble said, "the law is a ass," then history is a retard. To be sure my caustic tone is fed by jealousy and, why not say it, loathing of the purest order. What else could prompt these grizzled paws of mine to *tap tap tap* on the cob-webbed Olivetti I found in the attic of the animal shelter I now call home? Here I am, perched on my creaking hind legs, nearly twenty years old, deaf as a bratwurst, and in a tick-in-each-ear tizzy over the tomes of the so-called experts.[1] In

---

[1] *Hitler: A Study in Tyranny* (Alan Bullock, 1952); *Nazi Terror, English Tea* (Sir Nigel Davies-Wimbledon, 1950); *Only Following Orders* (Karl and Ilse Lügner, 1948); *The Rise and Fall of the Third Reich* (William L. Shirer, 1960); *The Origins of the Second World War* (A.J.P. Taylor, 1961); *The Last Days of Hitler* (Hugh Trevor-Roper, 1947); *Only Following Orders, My Foot!* (General Richard "Dickie" Webb [Ret.], U.S. Army, 1949). Together these litterbugs sully some 6,000 pages with their grammatically leprous clichés and platitudes:

When with solemn finger Duty beckoned, crumpets, cricket match-es, and randy birds in frilly knickers shall as childish playthings be set aside. At the docks it was, 'Cheerio, Charlie!' and 'Ta-ta, Tommy!' and 'Don't forget to write your Uncle Basil up in Wormwood Scrubs, he's so lonely, the poor dear.' And ere long the nasty man with the little moustache was hoisted upon his own bloody petard. For it is indubitably not the fate of the brave English soldier, he of recent green and pleasant woodland frolic, to risk life and limb to have pulled Europe's chestnuts from the Nazi fire with-out a song in his heart, a Flying Dustbin in his canvass bag, and a cup of strong tea in his belly. Oh yes, down at the docks it was laughter and mothers' tears and shouts of, 'Godspeed, m'lads! If we don't see you back in Brighton, we'll clink our pints in Heaven!' (*From Nazi Terror, English Tea.*)

every critically acclaimed doorstop I find her vile name. But where am I? Nowhere.

Who am I?

I was Hitler's cat.

Tutti Hitler. Male, uncastrated. White (tip of tail, black). Green eyes. Identifying marks: a faint scar on the bridge of the nose and a tear-shaped mole under the left eye. Born December 1943.

Or January 1944. That winter, records were not meticulously kept. If you recall, it was the time of our setbacks on the Russian front. The Red Army, broom-sticking our boys like rugs on a line, had recaptured Leningrad. The two vodka swillers, Vatutin from the left flank and Koniev the right, converged to surround our panzer divisions and … Ach, that business you can look up yourself!

I would not in any event have had a pedigree. Why hide it? So many tribulations has my Germany endured. Should I now, out of vanity, conceal, alter, and embellish my past? No. A humble beginning is nothing to be ashamed of: I was a mongrel bastard. My father? Never had the pleasure. My mother? A junkyard whore. In the year we were acquainted she bore seven litters, a her-culean achievement when one considers the typical ges-tation period for our species is 63 days, give or take. With her it was always the heat, and never a thought for feed-ing the mewling consequences of her insatiable lust. Once – I shall never forget this, though I could not have been more than a week old, eyelids glued shut – she bat-ted me right off her teat to make nice with the junk deal-er's tom. Another time I was sharing a wren with my brother Willi, when who should arrive to snatch away the lion's share but … Scheiße! I forgave Mutti years ago.

It is Blondi I hate. It has always been Blondi.

• • •

A man named Erich Kempka drove me to the Leader of the Third Reich.

Kempka was der Führer's chauffeur, errand boy, and (the historians somehow miss this) sock darner. Adolf Hitler, to my knowledge, never threw away a single one of his cherished argyles. All eight pairs – seven with "Montag" to "Sonntag" sewn across the toes, plus his lucky pink and baby blues for the days on which he declared war – were bought in 1924 following his prison release for the Beer Hall Putsch. In contrast, his secretary and cellmate Rudolf Hess was known to purchase up to thirty pairs a year, a show of extravagance that Hitler neither understood nor tolerated.

"Hess!" Hitler would pop off. "Am I going blind, or are those new argyles?"

Ever obsequious, Hess would bow his head so that all one could make out were the black caterpillar eyebrows he refused to pluck in the hopeless belief that "the chickies dig it." Then he would meekly mutter, "Sorry, mein Führer. The old ones wore out."

"Wore *out!* Gott im Himmel, what do you think *Kempka* is for?"

The Hitler-Hess sock tiffs were before my time. (The bunker secretaries, when lubed up with a little late night cognac pilfered from Reich Marshall Göring's locker, would re-enact the scenes with comic gusto.) Hess, as has been documented elsewhere, took it upon himself to fly solo to Great Britain in May 1941, with the aim of patching things up between our warring nations, and maybe picking up some more argyles into the bargain. During the final dark days of the war Hitler rehashed the failed mission with the top brass (minus Deputy Martin Bormann and Foreign Minister Joachim "von" Ribbentrop, sent for cold cuts and trapped for two days behind a Soviet tank unit). I purred in der Führer's lap as he conducted the meeting in the bunker sauna. His hands, as always, were as soft and sweaty as a baker's butt.

Hitler: "That nutbar Hess! Signs out our best Messerschmitt, parachutes into *Scot*land, insults the socks of the farmer who finds him, and *then* gets nabbed at customs for smuggling in an illegal number of argyles! What was it, fifty pairs?"

Heinrich Himmler: "Mein Führer, he had fifty-six pairs in his possession when –"

Hitler: "Fifty-six! *Verdammt!* I too love my argyles, but a man must practice self-control! What are we, Gypsies at an open bar? Hess was a junkie, plain and simple! In Bologna we went window shopping with Mussolini and ... Göring! You pigdog! Cover your mouth when you cough!"

Hermann Göring: "Sorry, mein Führer."

Hitler: "Spread your icky germs, and then 'sorry' like some hausfrau who has burnt the schnitzel!"

Göring: "The situation will not repeat itself, mein Führer."

Hitler: "You got *that* right – I'll shoot you in the neck if it does! Tubby, you gotta start bringing more to the table. Head of the Luftwaffe, and you couldn't even slap together a decent airshow for my last birthday! At least Hess *tried* with the English! Ach, it pains my

Aryan skull that we ever took up arms against our brothers in argyle!"

Josef Goebbels: "We should have formed a united front against the Reds. In fact, mein Führer, I'm of the opinion that it's not too late. With a little propaganda here, a big lie there, the Reds would not stand a –"

Hitler: "Cossacks and Commies! Half of them don't even *wear* socks! The others pull over their dumb feet a bristly, unicolored cloth better suited for making potato sacks! Now, the English may not have any back teeth, but it is only they and we who appreciate the simple dignity of a well-made argyle!"

Himmler: "Our spies inform us that Churchill wears his even to bed."

Albert Speer: "Rommel said Montgomery. Had pretty. Argyles. In Africa. Yellow-mauves."

Goebbels: "Remember Chamberlain's back in 'thirty-eight? Old Neville –"

Hitler: "How could I ever forget *Chamberlain's* argyles! The Munich Pact, turquoise and navy blues! And just the right amount of pant cuff to really show them off! Ach, why does life have to stink so much?"

Speer: "We could jack up. Production. On turquoise. And navy blues. The seamstresses. Could work. Overtime. Sixteen hours. A day. Maybe –"

Hitler: "Knock it off, Slowly! We're Kaputtsville! I know it, you know it, this damn cat knows it! Scheiße! Everybody spread out! I need some lebensraum! Himmler, help Göring up – what a porker! Slowly, bring me Blondi, and Goebbels, take this damn cat outta here! I gotta think!"

If only I had a tin of sardines for every time "Slowly,

bring me Blondi, and Goebbels, take this damn cat outta here!" stabbed my earholes like a sharpened pencil. On top of that, Goebbels's hands, which his long-suffering wife and many mistresses could have corroborated, were as cold and hard as a meat packer's butt.

And yet, and yet. There were times when Hitler showed me the utmost kindness. Charisma oozed from the man like pulp from a sledgehammered pumpkin. When he tickled his bristly moustache against my nose-holes, coupled with a bit of chin-stroking and a mesmerizing look from his eyes, blue as an old nurse's varicose veins, I would completely forget that no one had changed my litter box in weeks. This element of his character, a mercury stream elusiveness, was what kept me from cranking out this memoir until now (1962, and where have the years gone?).

I mean, I knew Adolf Hitler. I slept on his feet. I yowled like an air raid siren when, during fitful nightmares, he would kick me in the face (by accident, all 82 times, but alas never an apology). I witnessed his petty squabbles with Eva Braun and, at the end, their wedding in the bunker. I overheard him rip new ones for the field generals whose armies were being flattened like worms under rubber boots on a wet school sidewalk. And, of course, I watched him agonize as victory slipped inexorably from his grasp. But did I, ultimately, *know* him? No. On this point, I concur with the historians: Hitler was an enigma.

• • •

The first time I laid eyes on der Führer, from a distance of fifty yards, smoke was smoldering off his tousled hair and soot blackened his cheeks and forehead. Beneath the lazuline sky outside the Reich Chancellery, Bormann and an SS bodyguard were propping him up as he staggered across the grounds, as dazed and helpless as a retired librarian.

This was in the summer of '44. My brother Willi and I, who, despite our tender months, had been pitched by Mutti into the cruel world like gangster hits into a river, had since early spring been eking out an existence as homeless scavengers. When we heard the detonation, from inside an overturned trash can in an alley off Leipzigerstraße (just a block away), our first reaction was, "The Yanks dropped a doozy! Let's go looting!"

In fact, Ike's carpet bombers had not struck. The blast signaled the resounding failure of the July 25 Exploding Cigar Plot, which flopped close on the heels of the July 20 Bomb Plot, July 12 Razor in the Apple Plot, and July 7 When He Comes in We Shine the Flashlight in His Eyes and Shout "Boo!" Plot. Hitler, like one of those perversely resilient felines in a cat and mouse cartoon, seemed destined to be blown up, poisoned, and scared to within an inch of his life over and over again – only to pick himself up off the ground, get Bormann to dust him off, and come back for more.

Our disappointment at finding no victuals was crushing. Willi, fur and bones like me, whimpered dejectedly for a while before declaring, "That *tears* it! I'm hitting the road, Brother. North, south, east, west, I'm going to where they'll treat me best! Deutschland's got nothing to offer decent cats like us. Are you with me?"

I was, and remain, a patriot. Willi and I gave each other one last, bittersweet tongue bath. Then I bade him farewell.

A lifetime would pass before I was reunited with my closest friend in the world.

· · ·

On New Year's Day 1945, I awoke hungover on cat-nip (a youthful addiction I kicked long ago). The bass drum solo thumping in my head did not prevent me from noting the black limousine parked on Bergmannstraße, in front of Tenzer's fish market. Tenzer was okay, but his wife used to swat me with a ping-pong paddle when she caught me ransacking her garbage. Once she dropped a mitten by the curb, and Willi and I sprayed it. Really drained the old bladders. When she retrieved the damp mitt a minute later, she sniffed it, made a face, and pulled it over her bloated fin-gers. Still another time we clashed over some carp heads that … Scheiße! Look at me wasting typewriter ribbon on fat Frau Tenzer! Kempka! Back to Kempka!

The sun, weak though it was, flickered on the limo's waxy hood like the sequined tassels on a jiggler's jugs. I thought, *This is my chance.* At what, I could not have said, but I was, despite my Oliver Twistish kittenhood, a dreamer.[2]

Erich Kempka, gigolo-strutting below a brilliantine sculpted black pompadour, emerged from the fish mar-ket. He wore a black leather uniform, crisp white shirt, brass buttons, gold cufflinks, black leather gloves, and a burgundy ascot (untied). His bearing struck me as

---

[2] By the bye, Charles Dickens's tale of the woeful orphan is the only novel I ever read twice. Normally I fancy my prose in the newspaper mode, a habit I acquired back when I was unwrapping fish bones in dumpsters all over Berlin's gritty south side.

somber, imperturbable, and swanky – a French minister at a state funeral. In the crook of his left arm he held a pungent bundle, the contents of which, to your correspondent's finely-honed noseholes, were in no doubt: trout.

Kempka withdrew a set of tinkling keys from his pants pocket, and unlocked the driver's door. He was humming a passage from Wagner's *Lohengrin* (in my opinion, the Bayreuth maestro's best). The dapper chauffeur leaned into the back seat and laid down the catch of the day. I leapt in unnoticed, and hid myself under the front seat. How daring I was then! A young delinquent, close to starving, tough as a jackboot, and taking risks like there was no tomorrow. Picture Jimmy Cagney in *The Public Enemy*.

The limo wove its way through the bereaved avenues of Berlin. Kempka, redolent of ritzy aftershave lotion, drove with an unhurried lordliness, neatly missing the potholes that pockmarked the roads of our bombarded city. Soon he switched from Wagner to Edith Piaf, and belted out, with soul-wrenching melancholy, hit after hit by the Little Sparrow. During "J'ai Dansé avec L'amour" I cloak-and-daggered it to the back seat, and binged on the trout. I ate only four of the five fish there: first, because I did not want to be greedy, and second, after four my gut had puffed up like the Hindenburg, and oh the humanity I feared that I too would burst.

Soon Kempka pulled into the parking lot over the bunker, the gravel beneath the limo's tires crunching and kvetching like an uncle eating stale bread. I was stretched out on my side, belly distended, and licking my paws like a Dutchman. Breakfast had been exquisite, the trout complemented sublimely by the chauffeur's mellifluous pipes.

A sudden, heart-stopping click of an opened car door, and I snapped out of my reverie. Like Goldilocks discovered in Baby Bear's bed, I was do-si-doing in a puddle of my own sweat. But I was no silly broad lost in the woods. No crying, screaming, or tugging fistfuls of curly yellow hair out of *my* scalp. I had my wits, thank you very much:

Brain locked on point-form. Jerked up into crouch position. Nails out and back arched means *back off!* Through limo windows, panorama'd the scenery. Bipeds, maybe twenty. SS uniforms. Armed, unsmiling. Cat lovers? Would guess not. No trees for upward escape. Size limitations prevented view of ground. Any case, no chance we had parked amidst camouflaging vegetation. Pray? Forget it (atheist). Plan? Improvise.

Well, *that* was settled!

Then, in what seemed an eternity but in reality was perhaps only half as long, a large dog shot into the limo, scampered up the front seat, and, with fore legs hanging over the headrest, lowered her neck and *slobbered* on my face!

Blondi! That ignorant bitch!

In self-defense, I scratched at her eyeballs and snout.

She froze, as perplexed as a Pole who has been handed a book for his name day.

Less menacingly, she again hung her bulky duffel bag of a head down, and dripped saliva over me anew. In a matter of seconds she had killed the trout scent that I had so painstakingly licked over myself!

I remained stock still, playing the old wait-and-see, and resigned myself to the dismayingly wet inspection.

All at once she bared her teeth, exhaled nasty doggie

breath, and opened her mouth wide, in plain anticipation of making a morsel of my whole head!

So *that* was how it was going to be!

Now I called upon my reserves of fury. I slashed left and right, high and low, hissing and clawing like a cornered Serb, while bobbing and weaving from her bunglesome attempts to snap my noggin off. I drew blood from her mouth, and then clipped her jaw, and then – *bingo!* – a deep gash in the corner of her right eye.

She winced, and her eye began to close, but to my horror the pneumatic moron would not relent! So I worked the eye, left jab, left jab, left jab, no mercy, just pounded it like a stubborn mule – all to no avail. In the back of my mind was planted the grisly notion that I could not keep it up much longer, that my strength was deserting me like a protectorate puppet governor when the going got tough.

Then, at the moment I thought myself as lost as Amelia Earhart sputtering over the Pacific, Fate intervened, and I was spared the ignominy of being eaten alive by an inferior beast. Kempka reached in and yanked the dog out by her metal-studded collar. After passing Blondi off to Goebbels, he peered into the car. "Mein Gott! It's a cat!"

Maintaining my defensive pose, I hoped to strike fear into any other potential foe; but it was all a charade. I was done fighting, and struggled just to retain consciousness, not to mention control over my chockablock bowels.

Just then a dark blonde lady in her early thirties, with forearm shading brow, gazed angelically into the window. "Poor little guy!"

From the other side of the vehicle came a voice I would later come to know all too well. "Step aside, Eva. I'm reaching for my revolver."

"Hermann Wilhelm Göring! You put that gun away, *now!*"

With that, Fräulein Braun opened the door, bent down, and lifted me from the limo. I went limp in her arms. She pressed me to her bosom and carried me underground.

I Meet Adolf Hitler

After the war broke out, Hitler built the bunker as part of a buy two, get one free deal he went in on with the bespectacled Himmler and chunky Göring (the latter, with characteristic improvidence, installed on his Carin Hall estate, in the woods northeast of Berlin, not only a bunker but an accordion-shaped swimming pool). The current uses of the subterranean lodgings, as bomb shelter and communications center after the deep-frying of the nearby Reich Chancellery, supplanted an altogether different role.

The bunker was originally constructed to house overnight meetings, ostensibly brainstorming pow-wows but in fact nights away from the old ball and chains. Nazi wives were notorious for their nagging, and a dressing-down compositely drawn would go something like, "Ach, Mr. Hotshot Nazi! Home from the front. No time for the wife and kids, huh? But when you're mopey as a swing set in January, who do you turn to for snuggles? Who do you cry to, you goose-stepping pansy, when the Reds squash your little tankies like so many turreted roaches? Hitler, or me? Huh? Hitler, or ... Don't turn your back on me when I'm talkin' to you, Buster!"

"Das Klubhaus" provided the boys with a venue in which to let off steam. If one lent credence to the reminiscences of Goebbels and Bormann, the bashes here made the parties at Gatsby's West Egg digs look like Granny's 90th at the home. There were movie nights (der Führer's tastes leaned toward Nazi torture footage and *Casablanca*), chug-a-lug contests, oompah bands, tranny shows, line after line of Columbian blow, and performances by someone called Vulgäro the Magician (curtain closer: pulling a hat out of a rabbit). And, of course, there were the séances (Bismarck, Frederick the Great, and Peter Lorre were the most frequently called-on spirits).3

The bunker sat some fifty feet below ground. It was divided in two, connected by stairs that descended from the first to the second part. The former, with gray walls and linoleum floors, housed Kempka, the guards, the

---

3 Lorre, the obscene caller-voiced character actor, was pulse-wise still alive. He was Hitler's favorite thespian, particularly as Uguarté, the bug-eyed, slimy, exit visa-peddling hustler in the above-mentioned Casablanca (he also portrayed the bug-eyed, slimy psycho killer in M, and the psycho killer's bug-eyed, slimy sidekick in Arsenic and Old Lace). Lorre had fled to America at the onset of Nazi rule, along with one or two other Deutsch show bizzers, including Billy Wilder, Max Ophüls, Otto Preminger, Fritz Lang, Kurt Weill, and Marlene Dietrich. Once ensconced in his Hollywood mansion, Lorre found he had to switch to an unlisted number in response to der Führer's persistent phone calls. "Come on, do Uguarté," Hitler would plead, before launching into his own imitation. "'Heylo, Reek! You deezpize me, don't you? Bet why? Oh, you object to thee kind of business I do, huh? Bet theenk of all those poor refugees who would rot in theese place if I deed not help them.'" There followed the successful attempts to contact Lorre via the hocus pocus route, complete with burning incense, spine-tingling theremin notes, and first-class Maui Wowie. Then, to Hitler's chagrin, and the bafflement of the bracelet-rattling, babush-ka-wearing Nazi medium, Lorre managed to work out a system whereby incoming messages were re-directed to his next-door neighbor. Hitler went ape-scheiße, for Lorre's fellow actor, Jerome "Curly" Howard of The Three Stooges, was detested by der Führer for his Jewishness, unseemly slapstick humor, and, most of all, the high-pitched, ear-splitting manner in which he answered the tran-scendental summonses: "Woo-woo-woo-woo-woo-woo-woop!"

secretaries, the cook, and the maid, as well as Frau Goebbels and her six or eight children. The difficulty in ascertaining the number of Goebbels brats lay in the fact that they sported the same bowl haircuts, dressed in identical brown shirts with lederhosen and green suspenders, and all had names beginning with 'H' (when it came to smooching Hitler's popo, only Bormann's nose out-browned the Propaganda Minister's). In any case it would have been impossible to do a head count, considering how crowded the quarters were, and that the little monsters darted about like a Greek waiter's sperm under a microscope lens. Allowances must also be made for my dizziness in their presence, for they enjoyed flipping me in the air (they kept track of the percentage of my landings which were four-pointers).

Behind Hitler's back the people who lived in the first area peevishly dubbed it "the Bergen-Belsen Motel." The B-B was cramped, poorly ventilated, and badly lit (swinging by a black cord in each room was a brow-beating Gestapo interrogation bulb). The lone toilet, shared by some two dozen flushers, constantly broke down from overuse. The shower nozzle lacked pressure, especially for hot water. In addition to the bathroom were a huge bedroom (with more than twenty cots), a storage room, lunchroom, and kitchen.[4]

The second part, the "Four Star," was more like it: a classier smell, hand inlaid parquet floors, and walls decorated with paintings looted by Göring from the museums and private collections of occupied countries.

---

[4] Myth-buster: Hitler a vegetarian? Do not make me laugh, I might cough up a hairball. Where the so-called historians get their "information" I cannot say, but surely they never had Hitler tear off a strip of bacon from his BLT and let them nibble it out of his hand.

A buttermilk-fed Rubens minx hung in the First Couple's bedroom in the southeast corner. Bordering this room were Hitler's study, anteroom, and private bath (the last, done up in Chinese red, was off-limits to all, even his paramour). Beyond these were Fräulein Braun's many-mirrored dressing room, and the rumpus room (waiting in vain for the pitter-patter of Hitler's own personal jugend). There were also men's and women's bathrooms, a telephone room, map room, sauna, weight room, library, and one more bedroom, furnished with a bunkbed for der Führer's pet flunkies, Goebbels and Bormann (the latter, yielding to his bunkie's bad foot, on top).

. . .

In the garden, Fräulein Braun put me down, pulled open a hinged trap-door, and picked me up again. She climbed down a spiral staircase (which led to the second part of the bunker; the entrance for the unfortunates dwelling in the first was without rainbow-colored wallpaper and bowls, laden with nuts, set out at the landings). For the next two hours she kept me in the rumpus room, rolling crayons, tennis balls, and toy mice at me. I have always found these kinds of activities tedious at best, demeaning at worst. Still, I managed to feign interest. I even pulled off a pratfall or two to elicit some giggling from her. You may smirk, but *damn it* the woman had saved my life!

When she brought me a saucer of cream, I slurped it up. She hiked up her skirt and knelt next to me. "Poor little guy. Poor, poor little guy," she cooed.

She began to pet me, caressing first my shoulders

and head, and then massaging my hindquarters. Normally I do not like to be touched when dining, but the lady's hands were as smooth and nimble as a ballerina's butt.

"Ach, poor little guy. What will we do with you, eh?"

Keep pumping cream into me, I thought, without lifting my snout from the saucer.

"Poor little guy," she repeated for the umpteenth time. Really, she was not bright. "Maybe ... Oh, but he has Blondi. *Won*derful Blondi. 'Why can't you be more like Blondi, Liebchen?' Ach, I think he loves her more. He never forgot *her* birthday! 'Sorry, Liebchen. Slipped my mind. Busy busy busy. H_2 needed my input on the POW sleepwear. Pajamas? Nightgowns? Nightshirts? T-shirts? We went with the nightshirts. I don't know, what do you think?' What did I think? I cried for three days, *that's* what I thought! But that's it! *You'll* be my birthday present!"

She scooped me up and squeezed me like a Bavarian clutching his first brew of the weekend. I nearly heaved up the cream and trout!

"Tutti!" she shrieked. "My little Tutti! We'll feed you fish and chicken and ham, anything your little heart desires! How's that sound, Tutti?"

The name grated, to put it mildly. I grant that my street handle, Erwin, lacked the grandeur befitting a führer's pet. Still, Tutti? A lap dog's name if I ever heard one. How about something a tad more butch? Dieter, maybe, or Wolfgang?

The rest of the proposition, to be sure, was top-notch.

Fräulein Braun escorted me to the bunker library. At the door she hesitated a second before knocking three times.

Inside the room, someone hissed, "Scheiße!" That voice! How many times had I heard it ranting frothily on the radio, like a coach at halftime whose charges are being thrashed by an outfit of circus chimps! "Göring!" came the voice again. "If that's you with some more of your wife's satanic strudel, so help me *Gott* it's the firing squad for your big fanny!"

"Dolfi, it's me," Fräulein Braun sang out. "You two done yet?"

"Eva! You *know* my schedule! Ten more minutes! *Verdammt!*"

Fräulein Braun sighed and glanced skyward, the "can-you-believe-this-guy?" take. Then, carrying me adroitly in one arm, she turned the doorknob and sashayed into the room like a finishing school debutante. "Hello, Dr. Schadenfreude."

A gray-bearded man, facing the door, nodded coolly at my sponsor. He sat in a black leather chair, legs crossed like a Czech strumpet, fountain pen in one hand, notepad in the other. A shot of schnapps rested on the coffee table before him.

Next to the man, glowering at the far wall, lay the Leader of the Third Reich. The spectacle, even to my homeless-punk hardened eyes, was a shock. Der Führer, flat on his back, getting his head shrunk! He was lying on a couch, also black leather (something of a fetish with the regime, I was quickly discovering), with a throw pillow clutched to his belly. "Ach, what is it now?" He sounded exhausted, and made no effort to move.

Fräulein Braun held me away from her chest, presenting me as one might a fetching seashell recently dug up on the beach. "Look, Dolfi."

Hitler sat up and swung his feet, tiny-toed in pale blue thongs, onto the carpet. Pinned to his beige cardigan, over the left breast, was the gold badge of sovereignty – an eagle with a swastika in its talons. When he saw me his eyebrows quivered, and his face lit up like a macabre foreshadowing of the Dresden fire-bombings that would, in a month's time, claim untold tons of canned fish. "Keep it away from my argyles!"

Dr. Schadenfreude, palms clasped over his forehead in abject frustration, groaned, "Mein Führer, please! I thought we had moved beyond the sock fixation!"[5]

From there, things improved. Das Vaterland's first couple, vis-à-vis moi, reached a compromise, all due to Fräulein Braun's powers of persuasion (with one hand on hip and the other wagging a severe index finger, it was easy to see who saluted whom in this Teutonic duo). She promised to bar me from the argyle drawer; he issued an edict to all Nazi staff (read "Göring") not to shoot me in the neck. I thought, Jesus and Mary I've hit the jackpot! Little did I know there were clouds on the horizon, swooping in on me left and right like a Max Schmeling combo.

---

[5] The skeptics may scoff, but it was nearly two weeks after my entry into the bunker that I learned of Hitler's more infamous fixation, the Jews. Although I do remember the first breakfast. Hitler, while picking at his toast (whole wheat, plain), suddenly flew into a rage and began pounding a glass on the table. He said (or so I thought), "I hate the juice! Everything wrong in the world is the fault of the juice! We must eliminate the juice!" That he was just then holding a glass of OJ in his hand did not strike me as incongruous. After the war, when the full ramifications of the Final Solution were made known to me, I felt like a heel. With hindsight it is easy to pass judgment, to say I should have known sooner, should have done more, etc.; but those who were not there *can never know what it was like!*

First, it was my bad fortune (story of my life, let me tell you) to be adopted by Adolf Hitler just as the Allied Forces were crushing Germany like an empty milk carton. Why could I not have been born a decade earlier, when Deutschland was partying like it was 1999?

Second, and more maddening, was Blondi. She was aces in Hitler's eyes, and even if I live to be thirty I will never understand why. Owing to this inexplicable bent my life was rendered a living hell. I mean, Fräulein Braun kept her word regarding the cuisine, but – and *what* a but! – Hitler insisted on Blondi getting first dibs on every meal! Everything I ate for the duration of my bunker stay was soaked in her mouth water!

Then there was the matter of her "pedigree." I will be frank. Blondi was no purebred Alsatian, as she was so fond of claiming. To take one look at her you just knew she had some Doberman in her blood, maybe even Dalmatian. And of course she had to rub my snout in the fact that I was of mixed race.

Her conceit was surpassed by her near-perfect stupidity. The lapses in her general knowledge and common sense could not be crammed into Göring's size-56 pantaloons:

Blondi thought Leni Riefenstahl was a Belgian cheese. She pronounced "Speer" as if it were the sharp, pointy thing bushmen chucked at passing dingoes. She *liked* Frau Göring's strudel, and never turned it down, even though just a few crumbs of said pastry were enough to induce a three day bout of diarrhea in even the strongest horse.

She confused Norway with Normandy, Tito with Tojo and, most memorably, Stalin with Frau Helbing, the bunker maid. (Upon learning of his dog's attack on the hapless woman, Hitler had the *maid* destroyed so that Dr. Mengele could conduct a rabies test on *her* brain.)

She broke a tooth when, mistaking it for a pork chop, she chomped into Himmler's sidearm. (Hitler, true to form, held the SS Reich Leader responsible, and forced him to foot the bill after Mengele, again playing Dr. Fix-It, capped the fang.)

And finally, Blondi contended that the "Curse of the Bambino" was hogwash, and that the Red Sox would soon win the World Series. Sure, Ted Williams swung the wood with the best of them, and up the middle Pesky and Doerr were a double-play machine, but the *pitching!*

One thing was certain. I had not lowered myself from the gutter and into the bunker of the most powerful man in Germany to play second fiddle to some *dog.* Some dumber than average dog, at that.

Getting Acquainted

"Mmmm-*hmmm*, thass good eatin'! Tutti, yuh gots ta try some a this. Ah *know* yuh'd love it, boy! Nass, tas-tuh food. Not wet, no suh. *Dry.* Ah rah-peat, *dry.* Come on, haul yuh cahcuss on ovah to paradass! Yuh so close. So verruh, *verruh* close! Whutch y'all waitin' foah?"

Buford Pussycat Dionysus, washing down a smoked ham with a tuna juice chaser, beckoned me to join him on Easystraße. The invitations came in my waking hours and during my sleep.[6] They came fast and hard, ringing in my earholes louder than the fart bullets Göring pumped out after scarfing down half a dozen bowls of the cook's chili con carne.

The plan presented itself as clearly as the shaved space between Bormann's eyebrows. I had to get between Hitler and the bitch, and use everything and everyone at my disposal. Ruthless? Damn straight I would be ruthless. This was war, life and death for millions, but especially for me.

Fräulein Braun was in my corner, but where Blondi

[6] I will say it simply so that there can be no mistake: cats are not lazy! We take many naps, but it is only to preserve our physical strength and cognitive acuity. Think of a musical triangle player or football place-kicker, who, during most of the concert or match, is still and quiet, breathing deeply, perhaps with eyes closed, perhaps even lying down. Now think of a scorching spotlight, and of the raw burst of energy and calm nerves required to strike precisely with a tiny steel rod the divine "Drummer Boy" notes, or to hoof the game-winning field goal through the uprights with nary a second left on the time-clock. I trust everyone grasps the implications of my little analogy.

was concerned her sway over Hitler, like sparrows at a bay window, stopped dead. Der Führer, in the getting-to-know-you stage, regarded me warily and with a detectable degree of contempt, as if I were a burgeoning hemorrhoid that had not yet begun to pain. I was on my own, and would have to scratch like a bastard for every inch (what else was new?).

My toolbox was well-stocked. Hammering away with discretion and duplicity, I set out to fashion the key that would unlock Hitler's treasure chest of affections.

· · ·

To get the skinny on the supporting cast, I embarked on a reconnaissance patrol.

The bunker secretaries, Alice "Missi" Schmidt and Goldi Schettnopp, were an inseparable Mutt and Jeff pair. Alice, a close-cropped blonde with an ungarnished boiled potato of a face, was as long and slim as a K98 bolt-action rifle and bayonet. Short and plump Goldi, who at variance to her Christian name bore dark features and a bonnet of wavy black hair, was dimpled and lush-lipped. Hanging at all times from her neck, off a velveteen rope and resting atop her breasts, was a pair of horn-rimmed glasses (I believe as a kitschy accouterment, for I never saw her consult them).

I first came upon the two women in the B-B lunchroom during one of their ten minute breaks (which often stretched to twelve, even fifteen, minutes – it was the little things that cost us the war). As they puffed their Lucky Strikes and munched on confectionary bars, they debated the question of who was the biggest Nazi heartthrob.

Alice admitted to fantasizing about being driven deep into the Black Forest by Kempka, and there ravaged by him under the shade of a leafy oak. "I want him to blindfold me with that ascot and be beastly to me!"

Goldi, while not begrudging the chauffeur stud muffin status, said it was none other than Hitler himself with whom she was smitten. She took a long, sensual drag off her lipstick-smeared cigarette. "I've been having hot dreams – and mein Gott, Missi, don't tell *anyone* – of him loving me up!"

Alice's pale gray eyes grew big as two-mark coins. "Reeeeeally?"

"I guess I have a thing for authority figures," Goldi allowed, stubbing the butt into the ashtray. "And he's, like, *all*-powerful. I mean, if he wanted he could send us to Ravensbrück![7] Maybe I'm weird, but it turns me on. Plus, he's so clever. He got us back the Sudetenland for a song! He's a genius, really. And taller than you'd imagine. I think Leni shot him all wrong in *Triumph*."

The Propaganda Minister's kids were sadistic trolls whom I avoided like a roving pack of alley dogs. Their mother, at least, paid me no mind. Magda G., in her ratty pink chenille housecoat, spent the sunless days gulping tranqs with a "medicinal" syrup (the Rock-a-Bye Cough Cure). She mumbled mordantly about her husband's hussies and the scarcity in Berlin, since about '43, of quality chocolate truffles.

From the Goebbels brats I feared incurring minor injuries, and from the business end of Göring's revolver

---

7 The women's concentration camp, located about fifty miles north of Berlin. Several of the bunker's female staff perished there for what seem, in retrospect, patently minor transgressions: runny eggs, overstarched argyles, bearing a nebulous resemblance to a certain Russian despot, etc.

a fatal one. The cook, however, was the bunker inmate who frightened me most. Frau Schultz was a barrel-shaped septuagenarian widow who scowled like a pre-talkie movie villain. She greeted intruders into her domain as if they were centipedes found crawling under a soup ladle. The cracks on her square face, out of which half a century of zealously slapped on makeup could not be scraped, repulsed and fascinated me. She wore powder blue eye shadow and lavender lipstick, both applied in the thick style. The pile of hair above her head rose up in a threatening bouffant and was honey-blonde, a somewhat jarring color when one noticed the brunette follicles that sprouted above her upper lip. The black leather apron tied about her waist outlined, with demonically snug glee, the contours of her lumpy popo. She wore a haunted expression, with numerous facial tics, hollow brown eyes, and a wart on her forehead that appeared to be breathing.

On my second day in the bunker, walking about and spreading my perfume over chairs and table legs, I encountered her in the kitchen, standing at the sink next to a bubbling cauldron. Her naked elbows stuck out, the loose skin flapping like a basset's jowls as she worked. Then, *bang!* My olfactory nerves polevaulted a poultry vibe, and I figured I might score some spit-free din-din. Never having met the lady before, and wanting to mark her as a friend, I began doling out the free samples. I used the scent glands on my cheeks and at the base of my tail. After a good five minutes of having her mottled elephant ankles massaged and spritzed, Frau Schultz looked down – and promptly jumped back like a kitten catching its first glimpse of a mirror.

She dumped the chicken she had been plucking

onto the counter. Feathers clung to her gooey fingers. She grabbed a long meat cleaver hanging from a hook and raised it high over her right shoulder, two-fisted and glaring, like a woodsman facing down a larch, or his wife's partially-dressed lover. "Haw! Haw!" A giant crow recovering from laryngitis? "No begging! Bad cat! Haw!"

I went low, belly to the linoleum, and began to back out of the bad place.

She followed me. "Suffering succotash!" she added, and raindrops wet my head. Her dentures were stained and ill-fitting, and they wiggled up, down, and sideways when she spoke, and for a second or so after she fell silent, too. "Haw! Begging verboten!"

Begging? I prefer to call what I was doing 'making contacts,' but try explaining that to a lunatic who may at that very moment be hearing shouted directives from Herr Lucifer. Like a cappuccino-jittery Italian tank driver imagining snipers behind every bush, I put it in reverse and high-tailed it out of there.

• • •

Happily, there existed a few menschen to counterbalance the ogres.

The new maid, a sweet-tempered number named Fräulein Müller, preceded me into the bunker by a week (as Blondi victim Frau Helbing's replacement). She was quite the looker, in a Claudette Colbert sort of way, except for the long red hair and freckles, and welder's goggles she refused to doff because she had once seen a classmate lose an eye to some elastic-band tomfoolery. She also had – and was thus held in high regard by the popo-smacking bunker menfolk – a much plumper tush than the *It Happened One Night* star, and milkbags big and round as the M1935 infantry helmet (rolled-edge model). Kempka, the smoothie, was on her like zits on a mittelschüler. He regaled her with far-fetched tales that any non-bumpkin would have seen through in less time than it took Goebbels to spin calamitous defeat into cue-the-anthem victory (I mean, the phony attack on the Gleiwitz radio station – the one that pre-cipitated the Polish invasion in '39 – was masterminded by the fricken *chauffeur?*). When the new maid pressed him for details of his marital status, Kempka deftly 86'd it by serenading her with "I Lost My Heart in Heidelberg," a sappy World War I ballad that had even *me* swooning. Of the B-B tenants, these two were my favorites. They always had a kind word for me, some-times a little stroking or cream, and never, ever stepped on or kicked me. Love is a marvelous thing, and I wish it for everyone.

· · ·

I watched, and I learned. I scarfed up giant feed bags of information; some of it was digested for quick appli-cation, but mostly I stored it away like a constipated old Persian. I let Blondi gob on our food without complaint. I never went around Hitler when she was already at his side, tongue hanging out and barking ecstatically at his every move (did she pick this up from Bormann, or vice versa?). She attacked me once or twice, not so much out of malice as for exercise, but I discovered that a sharp claw jammed up her nosehole did wonders to snap her out of attack mode.

Our first real conversation, an hour after the brawl in the limo, took place in the telephone room.[8] Behind us, Göring was on the horn, hollering at a pizza delivery-man that "thirty minutes or free" had just been amended by official Nazi decree to "twenty minutes or summary execution." Blondi was eating a blue crayon, but she stopped when she saw me.

Blondi: "Are you Stalin?"
Me: "No."
Blondi: "Who are you?"
Me: "Erwin. Er, Tutti."
Blondi: "Are you a dog?"
Me: "No. Cat."
Blondi: "Kind?"
Me: "What do you mean?"
Blondi: "Pedigree, man!"
Me: "Oh. None that I know of."
Blondi: "I see. No pedigree. I'm an Alsatian. Bona fides coming outta my earholes. Mutti won top prize at the 'thirty-three Nationals in Hamburg, and Vati took second at the all-Europe in 'thirty-one. What's your mission here?"
Me: "Mission?"
Blondi: "Mission! M-I-S-H-U-N! Mission!"
Me: "Oh, *that* mission. I don't know. Fräulein Braun took me in."

---

[8] Like most cats, I am multilingual. I speak Cat, needless to say, and fluent Dog, as well as a little Bird, Mouse and Squirrel (for hunting purposes). Human speech of course lies beyond my capacity, although I capiche all that I hear. With each other Blondi and I spoke Dog, for she was as unilingual as an American – she failed even to understand "sit" unless someone pointed to the ground and pushed down on her back, hard.

Blondi: "Who's Fräulein Grau?"
Me: "Braun."
Blondi: "?"
Me: "Hitler's girlfriend."
Blondi: "Herr ... Hitler ... is ... my ... master."
Me: "Uh ... sure. If you say so."
Blondi: "Huh? Whazzit? Hey! Are you Stalin?"
Me: "No."
Blondi: "Who are you?"

This time I said that I was a swordfish selling ency-
clopedias door-to-door. After she gave a thoughtful nod,
I excused myself on the pretext that I had some spawn-
ing to attend to in the Elbe.

• • •

I was in the bunker three days before I saw "von"
Ribbentrop. He was standing outside Hitler's anteroom, a paperback in his hand. One of the
clotheshorses of the party (falling somewhere between
the flamboyant Göring and natty Kempka), he was
decked out in full uniform, all pressed and polished
and ready for his close-up. The sartorial effect was
marred, however, by the fact that he was slapping
himself silly.

I observed this from the hallway, perhaps fifty paces
away. An explanation for the Foreign Minister's behavior was supplied when, a few yards behind me, a closet
door wheezed open. Two heads edged out; the maid's
hair was rumpled, while Kempka's was neatly shel-
lacked. Fräulein Müller whispered, "Why's 'von'
Ribbentrop slapping himself silly?"

Kempka said that "von" Ribbentrop slapped himself silly prior to every meeting with der Führer. "You see, Boss hates it when the help doesn't pay attention. He really, *really* hates it. Example. If, during a meeting, you look like you're thinking of Frau Schultz's chili, like a certain Reich Marshall is wont to do, he'll bean you with a canteen. If you yawn, he'll put you to some demeaning chore around the bunker. And if you fall *asleep* ... Hooboy! Ever hear of Ernst Röhm?"

"You mean the former SA leader?" She straightened her goggles. "The Röhm Purge guy?"

"Ja, him. I was there, at one of the annual putsch reunions. Cruddy little tavern, the Buergerbräu. Wobbly tables. Red ants lapping up the vomit. Serving wenches looked like Goebbels in drag. Still, it was the poshest joint in Munich."

"Hey! *I'm* from Munich!"

"You don't say? Well, you can spank me later for that little *faux pas*. Anyway, it must've been June 'thirty-four. The big guy's going on for maybe fifteen hours about the socks. How the Slavs are inferior, wouldn't know a good argyle from a stuffed pepper, blah, blah, blah."

"Ja, what's the deal with the socks?"

Kempka shrugged. "Ask that shrink, Schadenfreude – that's why they pay him the big marks. I'm just the wheel man. But back to the beer hall. Boss is yammering on and on about the argyles, and everyone's eyelids are getting heavier, heavier. Finally Röhm passes out in Himmler's lap, and *Herr Gott* did Boss ever pitch a fit! Thousands dead! Röhm's SA buddies, his family, mailman, clarinet teacher, *budgie*, the whole kit and caboodle! Now they're all afraid of being caught daydreaming, or worse, so beforehand they load up on coffee and slap themselves silly. And 'von' Ribbentrop has it tougher than the rest."

"How's that?"

"He's narcoleptic."

"Von" Ribbentrop slapped himself one last time – savagely, on the mouth – and then brought up a thin knuckle and knocked gently. Hitler gruffly called him in.

"Okay, doll," Kempka said, switching gears from Nazi tour guide to slick playboy. "Show's over. We've got inventory to do."

The maid giggled. The closet door swung shut.

I ambled down the corridor and flopped on my side. The floor was wet and stank of fresh Lysol, but I let it slide. Licking out some dingleberries, I mulled over what I had just witnessed. That is, could I somehow incorporate it into the big scheme?

Then all at once I spied Göring blustering towards me like a one-man cyclone. The medals draped across his chest and the gold-plated epaulets glinting on the shoulders of his sky-blue uniform crashed into one another like a belly dancer's finger cymbals. The overall effect, however, suggested not slinky seduction but itchy agitation. He was sniffing like an auxiliary police pooch, teeth grinding, and rubbing the back of his meatball hand across his noseholes.

The Luftwaffe blimp came to a halt. The muscles in his neck cracked as he swivelled his head like a Spaniard limbering up for a penalty kick. As a recovering catnip addict just days removed from his last high, I recognized the signs in a fellow dope fiend.

When he saw me he cut the neck bit and flashed a sinister grin. He dug his revolver out of its hip holster. In an instant I twisted around and got up, but was unable to move. I was frozen at that well-known feline crossroads marked "Flee and Maybe Escape" and "Play Possum and Maybe Be Left Alone."

Out of the corner of my eye I saw the Reich Marshall break open his sidearm. With a pudgy forefinger he spun the chamber, faster and faster, with the guileless concentration of a kindchen spinning his new top. Then he plucked a silver bullet from his shirt pocket, simultaneously kissing it and winking at me, and pushed it into one of the holes in the chamber. He snapped the gun back together, lifted the barrel to his right eye, and aimed it at my neck. "Hey ho, little cat." His eyes glittered like demon sparklers. "How many jelly beans in the jar?"

Perhaps he was merely trying to get a rise out of me, the sick puppy, but I was not taking any chances.[9] I skedaddled thataways.

He lumbered after me, opting to hold fire until a clear shot presented itself. We stampeded through the telephone room (where Goebbels, murmuring clandestinely into the receiver, was dripping honey onto some

[9] Among bunker regulars, Göring was the lone practical joke aficionado. A "Reich Marshall Special" consisted of pointing his gun at someone's neck when it had only the one silver bullet in the chamber, shouting "Think fast!", and then pulling the trigger. Himmler and Goebbels got off with only soiled skivvies; fairing less happily were several guards, maids, and Count von Stauffenberg (the attaché case drop-off boy in the July 20 Bomb Plot, as well as the condiment sprinkler in the May 26 Too Much Cayenne Pepper in the Tomato Soup Plot). There were also wet willies administered with an index finger whose nail Göring intentionally left unclipped, and buckets of ice water poured on sleeping bunker personnel (usually Goldi, whose brustwarzen, to the Reich Marshall's chortling relish, would instantly swell and harden to poke pebble-like through her soaked nightshirt). Only der Führer, Fräulein Braun, Blondi, and the fearsome Frau Schultz enjoyed immunity from such horseplay.

floozy like a bee with the runs), back out into the corridor, through the library (Göring sent a shelf of Current Periodicals flying), der Führer's anteroom ("von" Ribbentrop and Hitler playing checkers), and finally back out into the corridor again.

I glanced around, certain I had lost the porcine brute.

Then I felt the tremors, footsteps fracturing the floor like Zeus hurling Tiger tanks from the top of Mount Olympus. I scooted into the women's can.

In the washroom I found a man down on all fours, regrouting tiles. He wore baggy white overalls. They were not zipped up all the way, and the lapel of a uniform peeked out, with a gold-on-black enamel swastika clipped there. The bill of his officer's cap likewise was astern, presumably to allow for unimpeded toil; it lent him the aspect of a low-grade burlesque clown accustomed to throwing, and catching, face pies. Before I could discern who it was, the door flew open.

Scheiße! *Him* again!

Göring, caught unawares, looked down. Vexed, he grumbled, "Oh, Bormann. It's you. Where's the cat?"

"Heil Hitler!" Der Führer's deputy shouted from the floor, his arm raised high and rigid as a telephone pole.

Göring returned a limp-wristed salute. "Ja ja, heil Hitler, heil. You look ridiculous, you know that? Where's the cat?"

"What cat?"

I was hiding in one of the stalls, the middle of three, eyeballing the action through the slit below the door. With the revolver still held out in front of him, Göring ignored the deputy and scanned the room.

Bormann wiped a splotch of white plaster from his cheek and asked, "What's with the piece? And *what* cat?"

"Never mind the cat," Göring said, still sniffing and rubbing but finally holstering the sidearm. "And stop talking about the cat! The cat goes on the list, don't worry about *that*. You don't boil buffalo hearts all night and then tell old Hermann there's a gas leak in the tent! Say, what are you doing down there?"

Bormann stared in befuddlement, before replying, "Ach, you know. The argyles."

Göring blinked a few times, then smirked knowingly. "Yawned, huh? Serves you right. You're a high school drop-out, so this is the job you should have been given to begin with, ha ha. And what about those secretaries and their filthy habit? Don't forget to empty the ashtrays in the lunchroom, ha ha."

"Stop bullying me, you fat dugong."

Göring's laughter vanished into the night and fog quicker than an Essen shop steward with twins named Karl and Marx. A menacing, barely-controlled barbarity now colored the land-bound dugong's tone: "Listen, you dashboard monkey. You will address me as *Reich Marshall* Göring! You forget, I'm second-in-command of this little shindig we call the Nazi Party. Check a program, they're in the lobby. And another thing. Been meaning to bring it up. I happen to know you've been tattling to der Führer about me. How I've been skimming off the war booty. Making up new honors to present myself with. Leaving work early when no one's looking. Oh ja, I know your game, you Halberstadt Iago. The enemy stares at your shoes! I should take the bullet I've been saving for that cat's neck and plug it into *your* neck!"

Bormann stood up. He was, with Goebbels, one of the shorter Nazis; Göring was a head taller, and about twice the circumference. The Reich Marshall stuck his gut out so that it pushed like a soft wrecking ball into Bormann's chest. The deputy managed a weak smile, and said, "Pfennig for your thoughts?"

Göring poked his paunch farther into the smaller man, until Bormann was trapped against the wall. "My thoughts? Sure, Marti. I was just thinking what I'd do if a big cloud drifted by, pulled its pants down, and everything went black. Black's a color. Think of it. Law and order, all semblance of civility, replaced by Aussie rules. The first thing I'd do is fling you to the ground like an old rag doll and pound out a bongo beat on your thick lackey skull. Something with a Moroccan flavor, five-four time, like when the moon goes rusty and the green grapes dance. You like dandelions? Once you were unconscious, I'd relax. Fire up a Havana. After the stogie I'd strip you down like a new Mercedes parked overnight on the south side. Then I'd sponge you up and down, oh so lovingly, in Frau Schultz's chili. And *then* ... Well, you can take it from there, Marti."

Bormann gulped, and in a low voice exhaled, "You'd *eat* me?" He dropped his putty knife, wrestled himself free of Göring's gut, and ran from the washroom. "I'm telling der Führer!" he cried. "I'm telling!"

Göring turned and checked his medals in the mirror, flicking plaster from the one he got for winning a frank-furt-eating contest in Hamburg (or maybe vice versa). Then, after rolling up his left sleeve, he pulled a syringe from his vest pocket, and spiked up. He whispered huskily, "Oh ja, that's the bonbon," like a Lothario whose months of wining and dining had just struck mushy pay dirt. "Come to Papa, sweet Morphine."

The Unkie took the edge off at once. The Reich Marshall floated out the door, jolly as a souvenir Buddha.

I stayed put in the stall, collecting my thoughts as I resumed my dingleberry hunt. Göring was a violent, unhinged drug addict, and I was on his "list." This was a matter that required some serious deliberation. I grabbed some shut-eye. Not because I was lazy (see note 6), but because my brain battery needed recharging.

In any case, I did not sleep for long.

Fräulein Braun swept into the washroom and, spying the half-baked tile job, pulled up short. After tut-tutting Bormann's amateurish handiwork, she made for the stall on my right. She slid the bar into the latch lock, pulled up her skirt, and sat down.

Two minutes later Alice and Goldi came in. Grand Central Station, right? The secretaries, wearing matching black leather miniskirts, handbags, and fishnet stockings, stood before the mirror. Alice leaned her bony backside against the sink counter and chewed her gum nervously. Goldi reapplied her makeup.

"We really shouldn't be in here," Alice said. "I don't know why I listen to you. We *both* know this washroom's off-limits to the Bergen-Belsens."

"Screw it," Goldi said. "The B-B toilets don't work. *And* der Führer told me just this morning what a great job I'm doing."

Alice nearly swallowed her gum at the news. "Ja?"

"Ja. He's giving me a big bonus. That is, *if* he can sneak it by the payroll guy. Anyhow, Missi," Goldi smiled, like a school girl with a secret, "I saw the chocolate truffles *you* got from Mahatma Propagandhi."

"Goebbels!" Alice made a gagging motion. "You can *have* the truffles, *and* the gerbil face, *and* the gimp limp, *and* ... Oh, hang on, let me read you some dictation I was forced to take this morning." She pulled from her handbag, and then unfolded, a square of paper with shorthand scribbles upon it. Holding it at a distance, as if it were rife with cooties, she read in a high-falutin tone that made it clear what she thought. "'Woman has the task of being beautiful and bringing children into the world. This is by no means as coarse and old-fashioned as one might think. The female bird preens herself for her mate and hatches her eggs for him.' Can you believe that? That's what *Gerbils* thinks of *us!*"

Goldi, looking askance, was trying to decipher Alice's outrage.

"It's sexist!" Alice blurted.

"Oh, right," Goldi nodded.

"Gott, he gives me the heebie-jeebies." Alice let her arms hang at her sides, and a death mask fell over her face. "You know. I'd even. Take Speer before. Gerbils."

"Ha!" Goldi's cry exploded in my earholes and made me wince head to tail (the old antennas had been bent towards the gals, with receptors on "10"). The raven-haired secretary jumped in on the Speer riff. "Ja. What's up. With the. Way. Slowly talks?"

"Who. Knows. And who cares, they're *all* small fry compared to der Führer. I think he really is sweet on you. I saw him ogling you when you handed him the updated list of tortured Russian POWs."

"Ach, he was genial enough today," Goldi said, "but yesterday he wanted to shoot me in the neck over a typo. Like, how many people can spell 'Ermächtigungsgesetz?'

Plus, I swore to myself after the Desert Fox: no more married men."

"Well, you can't say I didn't warn you about Rommel. Anyway, apples and oranges. Hitler's not married."

"True. But there *is* Eva. And that muttly doofus is playing him like a Victrola. He'll cave and give her that ring she's after. In a way I feel sorry for him. She doesn't know how to please him, anyone can see that."

Alice lowered her voice and tilted her head, just perceptibly, drawing her ear closer to the oversized mouth of her colleague. Then, like a hungry porch gossip in the vicinity of good dish, she asked, "Are you in love with him?"

"In love?" Goldi echoed dreamily. She crossed her right arm over her stomach, and in its hand set her left elbow. From the left hand an unsheathed tube of candy-apple red lipstick glared accusingly at the low ceiling. Goldi knit her brow and pursed her just-darkened lips so that her dimples showed. She tried to appear nonchalant, but was tickled with the softball lobbed her way. She was primed to step into the box, readjust her jockstrap, and swing for the fences. "Oh, Missi," she said, milking her at-bat. "It's ... a *complex* issue. I don't know if I'm in love, per se. Flattered? Sure. Curious? Who wouldn't be? And I guess a little infatuated. But ... " She gave a weary, what-will-become-of-me? sigh.

Alice's jaw dropped and her peepers stretched even wider, calling to mind the photographs of the Sixth Army Munchian screamers, their corpses baked like raisins and bits of lemon rind into the snowy Stalingrad fruitcake. "But?" Her left earlobe drew so close that it lightly smudged her partner's lipstick.

"But," Goldi continued, oblivious to all but the ball-strike count, "it's messy. You know, with Eva. That hatchet face. And this war, of course."

She stopped and craned her neck up at her co-worker, presumably to see where the ball had landed. Alice, realizing the plates had been abruptly cleared away, pushed back from the table and patted her still-empty tummy. "This *damn* war!" she joked lamely.

A slumber party of merry cackling ensued (Alice's laughter was forced, but Goldi, who had lungs like a yard-wide contralto, shrieked in earnest; it was hours before I fully recovered my hearing).

Goldi put away her lipstick and walked into the stall on my left. This whole time, in the stall on my right, Fräulein Braun had remained as quiet as a Catholic priest watching a hundred Jews being stuffed into a boxcar.

The toilet on my left flushed. Weakly.

"Oh, no!" Goldi cried. "It's overflowing!"

Alice rushed to the stall. "Let's get outta here!"

"Nein!" Goldi said. "They'll trace it to back to us! And then they'll switch our heads! Is there a plunger out there?"

"Ixnay!"

"Ach!" I saw Goldi's chubby, fishnetted knees plop on the floor beside me. Then came the splish-splashing as she pushed, by hand, the gunk down the toilet's throat. "Just my luck, it *had* to be number two!"

At the sink, Goldi scrubbed her arms up to the elbows with soap and water, and cursed her "stupid, *stu*pid life!"

Alice opened the door and peeked into the hallway. "The coast is clear."

After the secretaries took their leave, Fräulein Braun flushed (her toilet worked), and went to the mirror.

The murderous expression I saw reflected there did not bode well for me. Future disharmony between my mistress and master seemed all but certain.

Blondi and Stalin

While I do not profess to have any special insight into the workings of the canine mind, I did form a theory with respect to Blondi's preoccupation with Stalin. I arrived at my conclusions after an incident early in my stay in the bunker (and I challenge Konrad Lorenz to come up with something better).

Heinrich Hoffmann, a middle-aged man with hands as pert and muscular as a jockey's butt, had served from the start as the official Nazi photographer.[10] Always in full uniform for these occasions (he was "official," after all, and the dress code was imposed likewise for the official Nazi baker, hairdresser, and bug exterminator), Hoffmann paid frequent visits, first to the Reich Chancellery and later to the bunker, to record for posterity what Goebbels, employing typical bombast, hyped as "Phase One of the Thousand Year Reich" – a projection which fell short by, oh, about 988 years.

One cold cloudy morning, Hitler and Fräulein Braun stood in the garden with Blondi and a few SS bodyguards. Bormann lingered close by. His hands, dug deep in his trouser pockets, squirmed like crabs under a beach towel. This genital tugging, in its more muted manifes-

---

[10] It was in 1929, while working as an assistant in Hoffmann's Munich studio, that Fräulein Braun was introduced to Hitler. Love at first sight it was not. Der Führer took one look at the rosy-cheeked seventeen year-old setting up the reflector, and said, "Gimme a double chin, girlie, and you'll be wearing hand grenades for earrings!"

tations, evoked the talismanic pantomime of an Italian infantryman manipulating his worry beads; when more agitated, Bormann's increased fidgeting called to mind a tyke who really had to whiz.

As expected, no one invited me to pose my mug and meow "Cheese!" I settled in beside a Churchill snowman made the day before by some of the Goebbels kids (crass things they were, too: in place of Winston's customary cigar was a prophylactic they had filled with tap water, tied up, frozen in the shape of a schlong, and painted purple).

Hoffmann busied himself preparing the shoot, overseeing the construction of a giant backdrop while intermittently checking his light meter. Hitler and Fräulein Braun, wearing their Sunday best (between them some forty pounds of leather), shuffled their galoshes impatiently in the snow.

Blondi, I noticed, was staring hard at one of the soldiers, a lanky guard named Sigi Kreschmann. In her eyes I saw confusion laced with dread, enmity and, it should go without saying, idiocy. Then I saw her gaze swing quickly from Kreschmann to Hitler, to Fräulein Braun and to Hoffmann, around to her tail, back up to Hitler, then to some of the other bodyguards and to Bormann, to her tail once again, to me, to the Churchill snowman, and so on. For a full minute she appeared to be tracking the flight of some outrageously spastic housefly.

What the bitch saw were kaleidoscope reflections whose original image was Stalin, specifically the newspaper snapshot of him that Hitler had pinned to the dartboard in the weight room. Knowing the venom with which Hitler hurled steel-tipped darts at the photo, Blondi took it upon herself to hate Stalin with equal fervor. She sought out the Commie leader everywhere, with the idea of making of his head a giant glazed ham to wrap and present to der Führer. Right then, with her jaw clamped shut and aching to unclench itself in an orgy of flesh-tearing pandemonium, it became clear to me that, with the *possible* exception of Hitler himself, none of us was safe from being mistaken for Stalin: including me, Fräulein Braun, Bormann, the guards, the Churchill snowman, the dummy's own tail, and – I hate to put too sharp a point on it but it bears repeating – *me*.

Blondi charged at Kreschmann. The guard caught sight of her through his thick eyeglasses, and at the last moment dropped his G3 semi-automatic rifle. She jumped and sank her fangs into his throat. Together they tumbled to the ground. Her gnawing was loud, and indefinably lascivious. Everyone gathered round and watched, curious but strangely docile, as if the spectacle before us were no more arousing than Magda Goebbels lying in the hallway gripping her silver applejack flask, sozzled, naked, and unconscious.

Finally Hitler pulled Blondi from her prey. She barked and licked blood off her snout. She was unhurt. Kreschmann, though a recent recruit, had known better than to raise a hand against der Führer's precious "pure breed" princess.

The guard scrambled to his feet. His glasses hung off his face at a crooked angle; one of the arms had been snapped off. His lips were flaking, dry as an English pastry, and he licked them gingerly, as if expecting to find cuts there (he did not; Blondi was a jugular kind of girl). At last noticing his high commander standing before him, Kreschmann recoiled, and then slouched, so as not to appear insubordinately taller.

Hitler was glaring up at him in such a way that the experience must have felt to the guard endless and paralyzing, like reading a thick book on economic theory. In a tone rendered all the more malevolent for its creepy flatness, der Führer asked, "Name?"

The guard shrank a little more. "Siegfried Kreschmann, mein Führer."

Hitler requested, and promptly received, Kreschmann's sidearm. Without looking, he handed the PPK automatic off to the nearest person (Bormann, of course, who held it by the trigger loop like a sissy boy finger-tweezing the tail of a dead mouse).

Der Führer circled the guard several times while wearing on his face the dictionary definition of "crazy suspicious."

He stood before Kreschmann once more. "Blondi can sniff out assassins. That's a fact. Indisputable by you or any ten hook-nosed shysters. Who detected the cayenne pepper in the tomato soup? The moths in my argyle drawer? The tacks on the shower floor? She's *never* wrong. You're a turncoat. That's it, isn't it? Sent here to whack me by Stalin and his overgrown moustache. And tell me, who needs a moustache that bushy? He never heard of trimming? It's tawdry, is what it is. But never mind that. My moustache is classy. And I don't have to put other people's moustaches down to feel good about my own. That's not what I'm all about. I'm more interested –"

"Dolfi, what about the pictures? Herr Hoffmann hasn't got all –"

"Eva … *honey* … I'm busy … right … now." Hitler's eyes never left the guard, and he continued with no change in his level tone. "As I was saying. I'm more interested in the method by which you intended to kill me. Before Blondi put a halt to your intrigue, that is. Let me guess. With dynamite, maybe hidden in a sandwich. Or by pushing me off a cliff, where, defying the laws of gravity, I spin my legs rapidly in mid-air, for several improbable seconds, before plummeting down. I get smaller and smaller, until I'm a dot that lands with a soft thud. *Poof!* A tiny cloud of dust appears. Sound familiar? I bet it does. Or maybe – ja, this'd work, too – maybe you do me in by rolling Churchill over there" – he hiked his thumb at the snowman – "after me down a steep slope. He gathers momentum and mass, hotfoots it up to five hundred miles an hour and grows bigger than three Görings, before knifing me in the back with his purple schlong. You have to admit, soldier, it looks fishy."

"You mean the purple schlong, mein Führer? Little Helmut and Hedda, and maybe Hilda too, filled a rubber with –"

"Not the purple schlong! You! *You* look fishy!" Hitler's outburst cut the sub-zero air into a million itsy-bitsy pieces. Eerily, he corked his fury in the next second and resumed in his previous calm manner. "Well, Kreschmann – if that *is* your real name – what do you have to say for yourself?"

The guard licked his lips again as he silently composed his response. "Mein Führer, I learned a long time ago that a man can be forced to pledge undying allegiance to only one dictator. And *you* are that dictator."

Der Führer retrieved the pistol from Bormann, who began once again to twiddle his beads. Hitler nudged the barrel to the guard's neck. "Confess, or you're a goner."

Kreschmann closed his eyes.

"Confess, or you're a goner!" Bormann parroted.

"Shaddup, Marti!" To the guard, Hitler said, "Suit yourself, Kreschmann*ov*. When you see your buddy Joe in hell, give him a 'howdy' from me."

The guard grimaced, and, in a preposterously melodramatic fashion, cried, "Tell Laura … I love her!"

"Ja," Hitler snorted. "Like I don't have enough on my plate."

He pulled the trigger.

CLACK.

Kreschmann looked out through a squinting left eye.

Der Führer scowled, and pulled again.

CLACK.

And again, and again.

CLACK. CLACK.

Hitler turned and spat on Bormann's boots (the deputy thanked him). Then he pulled the magazine out, let it fall to the ground, and replaced it with a fresh batch of cartridges from his own coat pocket.

CLACK. CLACK. CLACK.

Suddenly, out of ideas and completely flummoxed, der Führer, in violation of Rule #1 of every known gun safety manual, turned the weapon on himself, looked cross-eyed down the barrel, and began pressing down on the trigger with both thumbs.

CLACK. CLACK. CLACK. CLACK. CLACK. CLACK.

"Scheiße! This happened the *last* time I tried to discipline someone!" he groused (Goldi's typo?). He flung the PPK into a snowbank and stormed off.

"Dolfi!" Fräulein Braun called out. "The *pic*tures! You can shoot the guard in the neck later!"

"Ach," Hitler grunted, and kept going.

"Oh, here we go again," Fräulein Braun said, following him for a few steps with hands locked on her hips. "There's just no appeasing you, is there?"

"Guess not," came der Führer's petulant reply.

Hoffmann, who had only to screw his camera into the tripod, peer through the lens and click now that the backdrop had been erected (a huge swastika-clutching brass eagle crucified on a twelve-foot high wooden cross), threw up his arms in surrender to his moodiest model. "And they called *Dietrich* a diva!"

Fräulein Braun apologized to her former boss.

Kreschmann dropped to his knees and wept.

Blondi studied the guard a moment, and then trotted down to the bunker after her master. Struggling to keep up with her was Bormann, hands jammed in his pants and waddling like a perverted penguin.

$$\bullet \quad \bullet \quad \bullet$$

11 January, just after midnight.

I polish off Blondi's soggy leftovers and head to der Führer's bedroom. Hitler, I know, is in the weight room doing bench presses (Bormann spotting him). Beneath a black leather blanket a snoring Fräulein Braun tosses and turns, no doubt tormented by dreams of Goldi swiping her boyfriend.

In the corner of the room, exuding horror at its spartan surroundings, stands a stately pine dresser, six drawers, five feet high. A heart-shaped, gilt-framed mirror rests on the dresser top. Stuck on the middle drawer, next to an engraved fleur-de-lis, is a decal – unremovable, or so suggest the swirls of fingernail scratches – bearing the words:

**Property of Monsieur Albert Lebrun
President of the French Republic
Do Not Steal!**

I pull open the bottom drawer with great effort (if there *were* a God, would he not give *all* his creatures opposable thumbs?).[11] Bingo! Seven on the first throw. I take out an argyle. Samstag, butterscotch and orange. I flick off a dead moth, fold the sock up, and push as much of it as I can into my mouth. The rest flaps out like a Ukrainian goat farmer's tongue.

Taking care that no one is tailing me, I sneak up to the garden and bury the sock.

In a shallow grave.

In the part of the garden where Blondi plants her soup bones.

[11] One more religious quibble: where in the Bible are the cats? How is there space for fifty million "begats" but not for a single mention of Nature's one perfect animal?

The Ranks Stand Tight Together

On the evening of 12 January, der Führer and the Silly Six assembled for their weekly TGIF meeting.[12] For yours truly, it provided a crash course on the cracks and fissures that, beneath the facade of Nazi solidarity, twitched like a tickled fat lady. The bilious, internecine back-biting killed any chance for anyone to let his hair down.

The boys met at eight sharp in the sauna, which blazed at a fur-curling 196°F. I sat in on the deliberations unharrassed, since Blondi, back and forthing it through the garden, was hunting down prospective Stalins, breaking only to defile the grounds with prodigious heaps of her doggie-do (and, I hoped, not messing with the Samstag).

The sauna was small, but homey. Bolted to the wall was a Degas, "Woman Drying Herself," that Göring had removed from the study of some Viennese paperboy (it is true what they say about the Austrians and culture). No one noticed that the woman drying herself was melting away before our eyes (a week later Hitler had

[12] By early 1945, the Nazis had bogged themselves down in a spilt Scrabble™ box of acronyms. The Big Book of Nazi Abbreviations was 3,010 pages long and contained 650,322 entries. It emerged during the course of events described here that no one knew what the letters TGIF stood for. Hitler asked for clarification on the matter. There followed much throat-clearing and floor-watching. Then came the guesses, all sycophantic. This Germany Is Fabulous (Goebbels). Them Greatbrits Is Finished ("von" Ribbentrop). The God Is Führer (Bormann). Thank God It's Führer (Bormann again).

the painting trashcanned, exclaiming, "How'd *that* get in here? I *hate* Dali!"). Three of the walls were outfitted with wooden benches. I lay by the door, under the fold-up chair Goldi sat on to take minutes. I was doing the classic cat bit where I stared as if comatose, when in fact I was sponging up info like Göring's undershirt soaked up sweat gravy.

Hitler took the spot opposite the door. Only he occupied this bench, which had behind it a small black-board whose ledge was stocked with chalk and erasers. Except for Goldi, who had body issues, everyone was clad in towels (filched, to go by the embroidered logos, from the Savoy Hotel in Prague), and of course the obligatory argyles.

On der Führer's immediate left sat Göring, looking like a Sumo wrestler gone to seed, then Himmler, and Speer by the door. To his right were Goebbels, Bormann, and "von" Ribbentrop.[13] After Goldi finished mixing, and then pouring out, a shaker of dry martinis, the meeting commenced.

Hitler: "Thanks, Goldi. That hits the spot. Cripes, it's hot in here!"

---

[13] A thumbnail portrait of the six Nazi "sons" who, like Lear's daughters, scrambled for their fickle patriarch's blessings. Göring, the eldest, was a spoilt tub of guts who coasted on his First World War fighter pilot heroics and winning smile, a monstrous amalgam of Caligula, Louis the Sun King, and Toad of Toad Hall. "Von" Ribbentrop was the envious son, a civil servant-type whose affecta-tions of raised-pinkie refinement fooled no one (he had won the "von" in a raffle in 1920, and was always consulting his copy of Increase Your Word Power Alliteratively). Goebbels was the zealous, over-educated, runty suck-up with a knack for slogans; Bormann ditto (minus the education and knack for slogans). Himmler was closest to Daddy, in terms of goals (German domination), work

Göring: "Ja, I'm already sweating. Is there any more ice cream?"

Hitler: "Boiling in here, freezing outside! I *hate* January!"

Bormann: "It's July in Australia."

Hitler: "What?"

Speer: "I think Marti. Means. It's *summer*. In Australia."

Hitler: "Slowly, I don't care if it's midnight in fricken Mongolia, I'm *hot!*"

Speer: "The heater's. Malfunctioning. We've been. Having problems with. The saunas. Produced at the. Ford plant."

Hitler: "Ja, 'quality is job one' my *granny!* Cripes, but it's hot!"

Bormann: "Too hot, mein Führer, much too hot. Shall I find the new maid and have her shot in the neck?"

Goebbels: "Only our true and wise leader knows the optimum temperature at which a sauna should be set."

"Von" Ribbentrop: "The rapacious rulers of the Russian regime would wilt like weary wombats in this hermetic heat."

Hitler: "Look, let's keep the popo-kissing down to a

ethic (indefatigable), and body odor (leather and pears). Speer was the queer youngest son with the strange. Breaks. In his. Speech. Brainy, introverted, and more likely to spend weekends in bed reading architecture books than perched atop a watchtower in Buchenwald taking target practice on the inmates, Slowly was too "far out" for the others to fear or belittle. (Although they occasionally called him "Septemberling" or "neubie," derisive terms longtime Nazis used for the host of members who joined the party after the September 1930 elections.) Everything the boys said and did was subject to a terrifying kind of binary judgement; waiting for a thumbs up or down from Hitler permeated every act with a nerve-wracking dread, like facing a hanging judge on a bad hair day.

minimum today. As it is I got more butt hickeys than Hirohito has kimonos."

Der Führer, after waiting a beat for laughter, stood and grabbed a piece of chalk. Posing like a fencer, legs apart and left arm up, he proceeded to sketch, in fluid stabs that attested to his one-time flirtation with art school, a slew of X's and O's; then, in bolder strokes, arrows aiming every which way. Discarding the chalk, he reached under the bench for his pointer. He rapped the board hard, twice.

Hitler: "Okay, ladies. Listen up. Our defense is tired, our offense lackluster. We've been losing yardage. We look like *rookie*s out there! So, I've taken the liberty of drawing up a new game plan. All eyes on the board! This is Warsaw. These are the Russian divisions. These are ours. And this is – what in *hell* … Hang on, let me erase that … Okay. The Reds are expecting sweep right. They *always* expect sweep right, and *man*, we fall into their trap *every* time! But now we throw something new at 'em. A little razzle-dazzle. Here's the line of scrimmage. We drop back like always, but instead of 'sweep seventeen' we – wait for it – *blitz*. I like the sounda that. *Blitz*. Trips off the tongue, don't it? We blitz here, here, and *especially* here. We neutralize their special teams by holding them off the field. How? We keep the ball on the ground. We *have* to – the Reds are killing us in the air, thanks to our Zamboni-sized friend here and the birthday balloons he calls a Luftwaffe."

Göring: "Mein Führer, that's –"

Hitler: "Shaddup, Tubby. The blitz. The Reds'll react fast, I guarantee it. They're a veteran squad, gone no-huddle since the Caucasus. Probably they counter with a three-four defense, or, if we're lucky, tank-on-tank. Either way, if we focus, if we stay away from the mental errors – what did we have in Minsk, ninety-three turnovers? – we'll regain control of the Polish capital. And *that*, ladies, gives us momentum going into the Danzig game next week. Well?"

Bormann: "Ausgezeichnet! Wunderbar!"

"Von" Ribbentrop: "Effulgent! Efficacious! Effluvium!"

Goebbels: "I'll get on the wireless! Victory is at hand!

Bormann: "Full-bodied yet fruity! I laughed, I cried!"

Speer: "The basic. Design. Looks workable."

Himmler: "The SS is right behind you, mein Führer."

Bormann: "Hip, hip … *heil Hitler!*"

Hitler: "Marti! Sit down!"

Bormann: "Jawohl, mein Führer."

Hitler: "And after the Reds are carted off the field on stretchers, we go west, young men! Endzone or bust! It's time we spanked those Yanks. In particular their mouthy coach, Roosevelt. Did you see that piece in *Der Stern*, where Rosenfeld called me a washed-up sauerkraut eater?"

Bormann: "Ja. Cheap shot, mein Führer."

Hitler: "I'll say. And hey, I like my sauerkraut – who doesn't? – but at least I'm not a cripple with a horse-faced wife! I mean, ver*dammt*, what kinda Zyklon-B was *he* smoking when he said 'I do?'"

Speer: "Zyklon-B. Cannot be. Smoked."

Hitler: "It was a joke, Slowly."

Speer: "Oh. How?"

Hitler: "Never mind. Now, I know last month

Rosenberg's paratroopers laid a hurting on us in Bastogne. Before that, they did their touchdown shuffles in Marseilles and Paris. But President Goldberg's gonna be in for a nasty surprise when he sees the ten panzer armies I'm sending to the Rhine! Goldstein'll fall outta his wheelchair! Won't that be funny, seeing Cohen flopping on the floor like a pike in a rowboat? 'Ouch! Help me, mein pony-faced liebchen! I'm a pansy legless crybaby and I can't get up!' Ha!"

Bormann: "Ha!"

Hitler: "Moving right along. This next item concerns you, Tubby."

Göring: "Huh? Me?"

Hitler: "Ja, you. Pay attention, Mr. World War One Flying Ace With Twenty-two Kills! Mr. Next-in-Command Should I Croak! Mr. Only Jack Hale Wears More Tin! Mr. Fatter Than ... Ach, I had a really good one, but I forgot it. Anyway, you once vowed that our warplanes would always rule the skies. But now the pilots tell me the Russian lines are harder to penetrate than a medieval chastity belt. And when's the last time we dropped anything on London? When's the last time we downed a measly Spitfire? Nineteen-fricken-forty? I hear the Stuka dive-bombers can't even clear the runways! They crash left and right like wineglasses on Kristallnacht! Care to tell me why?"

Göring: "The pilots are liars! My flying carriages are the most –"

Hitler: "Zip it, Tubby! I got my eye on you! You've been messing up *big* time!"

Himmler: "If I may interject, mein Führer."

Hitler: "Shoot, H_2."

Himmler: "Well, according to well-placed sources,

the Reich Marshall here has a suffered a relapse with his substance abuse problem."

Hitler: "What!"

Himmler: "The blow."

Göring: "Himmler! You four-eyed chicken farmer! I saw you skinny-dipping with Jimmy the three-legged leprechaun!"

Himmler: "What?"

Göring: "I *knew* he'd deny it! Well, I hired a private Fu Manchu detective. He followed you around on a red tricycle for a hundred years and made sand castle sculptures of your bestial undertakings. It's all there! On the beaches of Pluto! Let that be a lesson to you, Betsy! Don't throw meat at the hangman if you don't season it first!"

All: "?"

Goldi: "Herr Reich Marshall, can you repeat that last thing, about the beaches?"

Hitler: "No one's repeating anything! Gottdamn your fat soul, Göring! You're higher than Mount Zugspitze right *now*, aren't you?"

Göring: "This and that. You know how it is. Also, could you please tell your moustache to stop winking at me?"

Hitler: "Scheiße! We all agreed to go cold turkey on the blow after the 'Nur Sag Nein' campaign! Ten weeks of group therapy! Of listening to 'von' Ribbentrop blubber about not measuring up to his father's expectations! The with*drawal* symptoms, the halluci*nations* – I'd imagine Molotov creeping to my bed and groping my thighs!"

Bormann: "I had that one, too!"

Hitler: "But I stuck it out, fat boy! We *all* did – even

'von' Ribbentrop, that spineless pigdog."

"Von" Ribbentrop: "Thank you, mein Führer."

Hitler: "Göring, if this is true –"

Göring: "Himmler's been after the two slot for years! Oh ja, the chicken man wants to change the pecking order, all right. It's complete propaganda!"

Goebbels: "I had nothing to do with it!"

Bormann: "I saw it all, mein Führer. I'm a witness."

Göring: "Now *this* one! The janitor!"

Hitler: "Saw what, Marti?"

Bormann: "Saw the Reich Marshall tooting up."

Göring: "You and what army! Mein Führer, he doesn't have a high school diploma! Look in his files!"

Bormann: "Bourgeois elitist sea cow!"

Göring: "You could trade your teeth for magnets and you *still* couldn't whistle!"

Goebbels: "I also saw him, mein Führer."

Göring: "The gerbil, too!"

Himmler: "We *all* saw him. An hour before the meeting, in the B-B kitchen. He's not one for being discreet, that's for sure."

"Von" Ribbentrop: "The fact, mein Führer, is that Frau Schultz, by a fortuitous fluke, found him first, in flagrante delicto. The Reich Marshall said it was a special cyanide for the centipedes slithering under the soup ladle."

Göring: "Ribbentrop, you poncey champagne salesman!"

"Von" Ribbentrop: "'Von' Ribbentrop!"

Göring: "I got your 'von' right here, buddy!"

"Von" Ribbentrop: "Oh, *that's* classy! Next you'll be mooning me!"

Himmler: "The Reich Marshall did six lines."

Hitler: "*Six lines!* Even after the second Russian winter I never tooted more than three in a day!"

Goebbels: "And six this morning before breakfast."

Hitler: "Göring! The blow you put up your nose today could keep half of China wired for a year!"

Göring: "But China's the enemy!"

Hitler: "Nonsense! By that logic we'd send our surplus argyles to Rome!"

Speer: "But. We do."

Hitler: "Really? Since when? I thought ... Göring! Now you're *farting?*"

Göring: "It's the chili, ja. Anybody got a napkin?"

Himmler: "Scheiße, that reeks! Why do *I* always have to sit beside him?"

Hitler: "You and your chili, Göring! Cripes, you're more colossal than that woop-wooping Stooge we keep getting instead of Uguarté. How much do you weigh?"

Göring: "Well, I don't think —"

Bormann: "He's three-twenty if he's a pound."

"Von" Ribbentrop: "Two-eighty."

Göring: "Now you're all just being mean. Mein Führer, I'm expecting a call —"

Hitler: "Nice try. You're not going anywhere. Hey, I got an idea."

Bormann: "A really brilliant one, I'm sure."

Hitler: "Place your bets, ladies. Closest to Tubby's actual weight gets the argyles Lindbergh left behind on his last sleepover. Marti's got three-twenty, 'von' Ribbentrop two-eighty. Goldi, get the scale. Okay, I'll take an even three. What about you guys?"

Göring: "Mein Führer, the Geneva Conventions expressly forbid —"

Hitler: "Geneva Conventions!"

All (even Göring): "Ha, ha, ha, ha."

Hitler: "Good one! Now you hush, fat stuff, while we try to guess your tonnage. And don't go giving away the answer if you know it! And *stop rubbing your noseholes!* Okay, how's about it, ladies?"

Himmler: "Three-ten."

Speer: "Two. Ninety."

Goebbels: "What did you say, Ribbi?"

"Von" Ribbentrop: "Two-eighty."

Goebbels: "Fine. I'll take ... two-sixty."

Hitler: "Goldi's back. Okay, Tubby, climb aboard."

Göring: "Nein. I won't."

Hitler: "Stop pouting! Get on the scale, or we'll have a *Göring* Purge!"

Göring: "Fine, but I want my objection noted in the minutes."

Goldi: "Noted."

Bormann: "Move your foot a smidgen. And when's the last time you clipped your toenails? A little more. That's it. Two hundred ... and seventy ... four."

"Von" Ribbentrop: "I win!"

Goebbels: "No, *I* win! You said two-eighty. You went over. I was the closest with*out* going over."

"Von" Ribbentrop: "But we never said –"

Bormann: "Everyone knows you can't go over, Ribbi."

Goebbels: "I get the socks."

"Von" Ribbentrop: "But that's – it's a *pernicious perversion* – of a *parody* of a – *mockery* of a *miscellaneous miscarriage* of – of – of –"

Bormann: "Mein Gott, you're a blowhard!"

"Von" Ribbentrop: "Why, you little –"

The meeting degenerated into name-calling, shoving, and other sundry abuse. The crafty Bormann made off with the flying legend's ocher and chartreuses – but not before "von" Ribbentrop's formal appeal was rejected by Hitler.

Finally, tasks were delegated.

Foreign Minister "von" Ribbentrop would step up efforts to get Humphrey Bogart and Lauren Bacall to enlist in the Nazi Party, thus providing a morale boost to the German people, and a red face for the Yankee leader Hitler detested so much he outlawed wheelchairs and the word "infamy."

Propaganda Minister Goebbels would broadcast the silver screen couple's imminent arrival, along with the new ditty "I'm Creaming All the White Russians" (sung by Kempka, lyrics by Goebbels/Bormann, music from the Bing Crosby carol, a Swastika in Das Haus production).

Minister for Armaments and Production Speer would, by way of alleviating the rations shortage, put another trainload of slave labor to work at cranking out an even greater number of the four basic food stamps.

Party Secretary Bormann would secure more fresh fruit for the bunker (Hitler had pulled back his lips and asked, "Did I *used to* have so much gum showing? Cripes, am I getting scurvy?").

Reich Marshall Göring was given two days to confirm the downing of at least one enemy aircraft, and a week to drop five pounds.

Hitler then dismissed everyone but Reich Leader of the SS Himmler. On the way out, I heard Goldi gripe under her breath that taking minutes, especially in a steamy sauna with the malodorous Göring, was definitely *not* in her job description. "MBA in Shorthand, and from Heidelberg!" she grumbled to herself. "I'm *better* than this!"

In the hallway "von" Ribbentrop, still nettled about the champagne salesman crack, pulled Göring's towel off and absconded with it. Amid guffaws (and Goldi falling away in a dead plotz), Göring, quivering like 274 pounds of tapioca pudding, gave chase – but only for a moment, for it was clearly a lost cause. As Speer helped a revived Goldi to her feet, the naked Reich Marshall, with bean-bag gut covering his privates, came up to Bormann, and feigned a good-natured smile at his own expense. Then, dancing on the grave of the Marquis of Queensberry, Göring sent the little lackey reeling to the canvass with a sucker punch. Next he yanked *Goebbels's* towel off and wrapped it round himself. The astonishingly underendowed Propaganda Minister shrieked, cupped his hands over his robin's eggs, and ran down the corridor. Goldi, just up on wobbly knees, hit the deck again. Göring sauntered off in the opposite direction, singing the Horst Wessel song ("*The flags raised high / the ranks stand ti-ight together*").

Hitler simply shook his head and told Speer, who stood insouciantly over Goldi and Bormann, "Clean it up, Slowly."

Speer nodded, slowly of course. "Jawohl, mein. Führer."

"Herr Gott!" Hitler exclaimed, slamming the door. "I didn't know mosquitoes bit *one another!*" He sat down, took a deep breath, and looked my way. "Say, H2, what do you think of Eva's new critter? I don't like his face. Evil, if you ask me."

Himmler removed his befogged spectacles and wiped

them off with a towel corner. "Ja? I didn't even notice he had a face. What's his name?"

"Name? I think – Tuffi? Or Muffi? Scheiße, I don't know! I didn't ask you to stay behind to talk about some damn cat! This is about Auschwitz!"

"I figured. The Russkis."

"Ja. The Reds are coming. Armored columns of piroshki-sucking Ivans and Sergeis. Those big T34 tanks growling like Göring's stomach five minutes before Frau Schultz slops that hog. If my blitz plan doesn't take, then we have to clean up and clear out of Auschwitz. You hear from Mengele?"

"Telegram this morning. He wants Eichmann to stop sending the trains."

Hitler winced. "All those Bureau-4 guys are such dipsticks! How many pieces?"

"A couple thousand. From Hungary, I think. Mengele says they're backlogged, after the bombings last November. Don't have the gas chambers for so many."

"Who does. Look, H2, you're my man. Get out there and take care of it."

"But how, mein Führer? In one of Göring's planes? I'll be shot down in an hour, *if* I manage to clear the runway."

"Take the limo."

"Kempka too?"

"Kempka stays."

"But I have bad night-vision," Himmler whined. "And I get lonely."

"Hey! *Clean out your earholes, pal!* I said Kempka stays! He's got darning to do. If you want company, take the cat."

Operation Samstag

Considering everything that awaits me that Saturday –
the junket to Auschwitz, the sweet pay-off to a frame
job on a certain Alsatian bitch, and a much-needed
bowel movement courtesy of the bran muffin I filched
from Frau Schultz's pantry the night before – I sleep
well. In fact, better than I have in my entire down-and-
out life, for I spend the night curled up and purring
between the thoughtfully parted Kewpie doll feet of The
Leader of the Third Reich. (It's also my first time slum-
bering on a leather surface. I find it spellbindingly
comfy, and *hot*. Twice I awake with a stiffy.)

Hitler rises first. He extricates his legs carefully from
the blanket so as not to disturb me. I pop open an eye and
watch him. He is wearing only his jockeys.[14] With
Fräulein Braun snoring in the queen-sized bed, Hitler
stands at President Lebrun's old dresser and roll-calls his
body before the mirror. A few months shy of his fifty-sixth
birthday, he sees reflected before himself a trim, if unavoid-
ably pale, physique. His places a hand on his washboard
tummy, and slaps it approvingly. His abs are ripped; he
pats them down like a pediatrician checking Junior for
swollen glands. Looking for fat, he attempts to pinch an
inch, but cannot. Now standing in profile, he flexes his
biceps, smooching first the right and then the left one.
Visibly pleased with the results of his two-a-day work-
outs, he leans forward to examine his moustache. He runs

---

[14] The jockey/boxer question is an easy grounder all the historians, save Davies-Wimbledon, manage to boot.

a finger through the hairs. A look of worry appears on his face. Glancing over at the bed, he is about to say something to his girlfriend when he thinks better of it.

He opens the top drawer, takes out a t-shirt, and pulls it over his head. Next he bends and slides out the bottom drawer. He withdraws the lone Samstag.

Of course, he cannot locate the sock's sister. His expression warps, like a potion-quaffing mad scientist in a time-lapse photography sequence, from distracted to annoyed to frantic. He tugs the drawer all the way out and empties the contents on the floor. He does a double take at the clang of the Schmeisser pistol he forgot was stored there.

Fräulein Braun's snoring is cut short by the ruckus. She pulls the blanket up over her head, and tries to go back to sleep.

Hitler sifts through the argyles. After a few seconds he savagely sweeps the whole lot aside. He lets out a wail, an uncanny imitation of mama bear finding her cub mulched in a steel trap: "Aaaaamaaaah!"

Fräulein Braun springs out of bed as if dismounting from a trampoline. "Dolfi! What is it? Are the Russkis here?"

"Aaaaamaaaah!"

"The argyles!"

"Ja!" He is shuddering like a POW spending a winter solstice under the stars in a vat of freezing water, settling for Nazi science some questions regarding hypothermia. "The left Samstag!"

Fräulein Braun throws her arms around him. "We'll find the sock! It can't have gone far. Maybe the new maid mixed it in with the rags Kempka uses to wax the limo."

"Wax? Aaaaamaaaah!"

"Liebchen, please! Stay calm!"

"What? Calm? Scheiße! Someone's gonna *burn!*"

Hooboy, Blondi roasting on a spit!

Fräulein Braun whips on her bathrobe, picks up the phone, and sends for Bormann and Goebbels. Like genies, they materialize even before the receiver has been replaced.

"We'll find the perpetrators! We'll string them up like Christmas tinsel!"

"We'll shoot them in the neck!"

"We'll switch some heads, mein Führer!"

Hitler gives short shrift to their revenge fantasies. "There's no time for head-switching, you midgets! Get the guards! Wake the world! The sock is close by, I can feel it! We'll turn the bunker upside down! The garden, too!"

At the word "garden" I indiscreetly let out an ecstatic meow.

Four pairs of binocular eyes turn, focus, and zoom in on the cat. A suddenly very *suspect* cat. A "how-well-do-we-really-know-him-anyway?" cat.

I drag out a yawn, and bring my back leg up to scratch behind my ear. For good measure I yawn again, and then close my eyes.

Like a charm. Every time.

• • •

The guards in their shiny SS knee boots are dispatched to the garden, with Frau Goebbels and the small H's to lend assistance. Alice, Goldi, Fräulein Müller, and Frau Schultz get the B-B. Kempka takes the parking lot.

Fräulein Braun, Bormann, and Goebbels cover the Four Star. Hitler remains in his bedroom – with Blondi, of course, to provide him succor. As for me, I make tracks for the garden. A little bird tells me things will prove most interesting there.

Outside, I climb the Churchill snowman for a better view. Hustle and bustle all about. Congratulating myself on a job well done, I think, *Soon it will all be over.*

Then I spy Frau Göring, teetering on spiked heels and bundled up in a leopard fur coat so restricting it may as well be a strait-jacket. She shoves mightily to open the parking lot gate. Slipping a few times, she finally pushes it closed again after a violet Maybach swings in. The Reich Marshall is stuffed behind the wheel, ten pounds of dumplings in a five-pound bag. He has a foot-long cigar, lit, in one hand, and a big hunk of Belgian cheese in the other. Displaying impressive dexterity for a human beach ball, he is laying waste to both smoke and snack while steering with his belly. He parks next to the limo, opens the driver's door, and shimmies out. Glancing around, a bemused smile finds its way to his lips. The garden looks like Easter morning, the whole gang foraging for colored eggs. He asks Kempka, whose popo sticks inelegantly out of the limo as he checks under the front seat, what the hell is going on.

"Left Samstag, Herr Reich Marshall."

Göring laughs like a pixilated kookaburra. After telling Kempka to get back to work, he rolls up his coat sleeve, takes a syringe out of his holster, and harpoons a vein. When he pulls out, his smile transforms to a beatific, droopy-lidded gaze.

Most of the guards edge warily along the inside of the barbed wire fence, kicking at the yew bushes, eyes on the ground and tommy guns at the ready, as if the sock is an intrepid prisoner who has staged a breakout. *Fools*, think I.

One guard, happily, has a brain that would not fit into a standard issue snuffbox. From the opposite end of the garden – I do not want to be near the sock, lest I implicate myself – I watch him run his boot over the thin layer of snow that covers Blondi's bone burial spot. I aid him telepathically: *That's good. You're getting warm. Warmer. Hot! Ooh baby, that's it!*

The guard bends to his haunches, and brushes aside some snow and top soil. He jerks the sock free. Then he airs it out, making like a Portuguese fisherman with yesterday's underwear. A stickler for substantiation, he goes so far as to read the stitching across the toes. His lips form *Samstag*.

"I found it!" The guard holds the sock up high, waving his arm like a math nerd who knows the answer.

Everyone hurries over to the flapping butterscotch and orange flag. Magda G. sends one of her towheads for Hitler. Thirty seconds later der Führer is sprinting barefoot from the bunker with the entourage, the bitch included.

Expectant grins greet Hitler as he approaches the guard. I climb down off Churchill, to better witness my rival's stupendous fall from grace.

Alas, it is, like a world in which ham blossoms on trees, not meant to be.

When Hitler draws close enough to make out the guard's face, he stops abruptly. I, too, look at the guard. I see the chapped lips, and the black electrical tape holding the eyeglasses together. I heap obscenities on Lady Luck, that cold-shouldering skank.

"Kreschmann!" Hitler explodes. His eye pop out, ping-pong balls with blue flecks daubed on.

The guard flinches. He holds out the sock and says, hoarsely, "It was with Blondi's soup bones, mein Führer."

"Ha! That's rich! I'm gonna believe *you*, you pinko spy?" Hitler snatches the sock, reads the stitching for himself, and pushes it into his back pocket. "Sidearm!"

"Jawohl, mein Führer."

Hitler takes the gun and points it at the guard.

"But mein Führer, it doesn't –"

"That's enough outta you," Hitler says. He dents the guard's neck with the end of the barrel, and pulls the trigger.

CLACK.

"Huh?" The would-be executioner looks as if his gray matter has just been sucked out his noseholes with a straw.

"I apologize, mein Führer," Kreschmann says. "It's the same gun. I asked for another one. But the payroll guy wouldn't sign off on the requisition form."

Only half-listening to the explanation, der Führer suddenly brightens up with a hopeful smile. He has seen the spotty-coated Frau Göring, standing behind the guard. "Carin! Thank Gott you're here!"

Frau Göring gasps, hand covering mouth. Then, as haughty as a duchess who has been affronted with "Hey, Toots," she huffs, "I'm not Carin. I'm Emma."

Hitler looks bewildered all over again. "What? What are you talking about, Carin? I was at the wedding! I was Tubby's best man!"

"Carin was Hermann's *first* wife!"

"May she rest in peace!" Göring blubbers out of

nowhere. Nostalgia and morphine have tag-teamed him into tears.

"Now see what you've done!" Frau Göring chides Hitler. She proffers her bosom to her hubby, where he drops his boulder-sized head. He bawls inconsolably as his wife pats his massive subcontinent of a back.

Hitler stares at his purpling toes and mulls it over. "Ja," he says, looking up as the fog clears. "Ja, that's right. Carin was the actress. A lot better-looking than you, too. Gams like Betty Grable. Got any strudel?"

"What? You said you *hated* my strudel! That if I ever brought it around again you'd make *soap* out of me!"

"Cripes, it's not for *me!*" Hitler indicates the guard. "It's for Joe Stalin's boy!"

As it happens, Frau Göring has just baked a fresh strudel. Hitler takes it from her handbag. He unwraps the foil, scrunches it up, and lets it drop to the ground. (Only I notice that, a second after the metallic paper lands, it is scarfed up by Blondi. That dummy.) Der Führer thrusts the strudel at Kreschmann. "Chow down, soldier."

The guard slumps in resignation, and accepts the pastry. He repeats his curious request of the week before: "Tell Laura ... I love her!"

"Of course I will. No problem. Marti," Hitler calls to Bormann, who, as usual, is playing pocket pool at his side. "Jot this down in my planner so I won't forget. 'To-do: Tell Laura the Soviet agent loves her!'"

"Jawohl, mein Führer!" Bormann pulls out a note-book, and begins feeling himself up for a pencil.

Hitler screams at the heavens: "Bormann! Go to your room!"

Bormann walks away, casting hurt glances over his

shoulder like a beagle whose master has unaccountably swatted him with a rolled-up *Adler*.

Hitler again orders the guard to eat.

Kreschmann contemplates the strudel forlornly. He licks his lips – I have never seen lips so dry! – and takes a teensy bite. He gulps. In a flash his Adam's apple bobs convulsively up and down, like a foie gras goose deep-throating a fistful of fatty fodder.

Everyone, save Hitler and Blondi, steps back. The guard's face has instantly been washed over in a gleaming crimson hue. He doubles over, arms folded across his gut. His mouth opens wide, as if he is trying to swallow an invisible barstool. The noises emanating from his stomach are extraterrestrial, a lovers' spat between two Martians. "Please," he groans. "Shoot me!"

Two guards raise their rifles. Hitler glares them into pillars of salt and pepper. Kreschmann sinks slowly to the ground, writhing like a Tarzan villain in quicksand.

Mercifully, it does not last long. Perhaps another hour or so.

By then, Hitler has already vacated the premises. But not before directing Kempka to have the body sent to the lampshade guy in Flossenbürg.

Of Cats and Men

"Why so glum, Tutti?"

Fräulein Braun, after Velcro-strapping to my left front leg a swastika armband, was brushing out knots of my fur in the lunchroom. Alice and Goldi had walked in earlier, looking forward, I imagined, to a jolt of sweet nic, but vamoosed the second they saw Hitler's squeeze. This I knew only because the bristles had dug into me, and I had turned to see what had caused Fräulein Braun to prick me like that.

The red and white cloth armband, mandatory apparel now that I was a Nazi pet venturing out into public on party business, looked spiffy enough. However, rather than take my mind off the sock debacle earlier that morning, it made me think again of Blondi. It was one of *her* armbands. My hypersensitive noseholes filled with her stupid scent.

"Poor little fella," Fräulein Braun cooed. Oh man, I hated it when she cooed. I really did. "I'll miss you, too. But Auschwitz isn't *that* far away. You'll be back in a couple days. And cheer up, Frau Schultz whipped up a scrumptious snack for you."

Well, at least I would enjoy a meal that was not marinated in bitch gob.

Der Führer did not deign to give me a send off, perhaps because of my "evil" face. Also, he was busy conferring tasty accolades on Blondi. Not only for unmasking the "Soviet agent," but for what she had accomplished a few hours later. Supercop had caught a hedgehog licking cheese off a pizza box that Göring had chucked next to the trash cans.[15] Strewn about the garden were bloody limbs and spiney hairs.

Fräulein Braun, still making with her throat like an aroused male pigeon, took me outside. Himmler sat in the idling limousine, a map spread over his lap, a steaming pannikin of barley coffee in hand, and seatbelt fastened across his sunken chest.[16] Fräulein Braun lowered me onto the passenger seat through the open window. Then, blinking back tears, she tried to extract from Himmler a promise to bring me back alive.

When the SS leader pulled a face that suggested less than complete commitment to my safety, she admonished him. "Don't gimme that bullsheiße, H2! I'm not

[15] The European hedgehog (Erinaceus europaeus) normally hibernates from October to March. Reinhard, the hedgehog in question, was, like me just a fortnight before, drug dependant – glue-sniffing being his choice of poison. Once, when tripping, he repeated Archilochus's line: "The fox knows many things, but the hedgehog knows one big thing." "And what," I asked, by way of humoring him, "would that be, Reini?" He smiled as if the question had surprised him, and said, "If I told you, then you'd be a hedgehog! Don't mess with the natural order, Tutti-Frutti!"

[16] Although Nazi philosophy played up the superior Aryan physique (strapping, blue-eyed, blonde good looks), none of the top brass, in swimming trunks, would have turned heads. Göring was obese, Bormann small and puddingish, and Himmler and "von" Ribbentrop scrawny as Mexican bean pickers. Speer was the only tall one, but his solemn manner, thinning black hair, and permanent slouch called to mind an actor doomed by typecasting to play undertakers and concierges in two-star hotels. Goebbels, funnily enough, not only had thinning black hair and the schwanz of a ten year-old girl, but webbed toes and a crippled right foot (the result of contracting polio as a child). According to the law he himself helped implement, these physical defects should have seen him packed off to the euthanasia camps back in '39. And Hitler? We shall let Goldi tell that one.

one of your heel-clicking Gestapo bootlickers!" She reached through the window and fingered my ears. "You take good care of this cat, you hear? Tutti means the world to me."

"Ja, sure."

Himmler revved the engine, and we glided past the gate. I did not know what I was getting in to, but at least I would be loosed from Fräulein Braun's mawkish clutches.

• • •

Berlin's streets lay as lifeless as they had been New Year's Day when I was chauffeured by Kempka. Except to occasionally push his sliding eyeglasses back up the bridge of his nose, Himmler's hands stayed on the wheel, locked in the ten-to-two position favored by student drivers and socialists. I settled in for a long, uneventful ride.

When we reached the suburbs Himmler turned down a narrow, unpaved road. We had been travelling in circles for hours, I thought at first as some sort of evasive tactic to ward off assassins. After all, that is how Himmler's SS amigo Heydrich had bitten it in '42 – bombed and machine-gunned in his convertible roadster in the streets of Prague. As it turned out, that cautionary tale was not on my driver's mind at all. Old Four Eyes simply could not read a map. Finally he found the right exit ramp, and we were properly on our way.

The whole time, Himmler was quiet as a stone coffin. I wished he would sing to me as Kempka had, or at least switch on the radio. As for the bucolic charms of the countryside, there were none. Once, I got up on my hind legs to peek out the window: nothing but bomb craters, derelict army cars, and the odd foot soldier, cut off from his platoon and drifting like a tumbleweed in need of a shave.

Much later something did catch my eye, at the side of a road in a village in Silesia. It was a female cat, pawing frantically at a small pyramid of corpses.

Her kittens. I counted seven of the little guys, as mangled as the pizza box hedgehog. A second later, we had passed them by.

Deep-rooted memories sprang up into my consciousness like the flying punchline from a snake mustard jar. Was it the somnolent effect of the waterbed-lilting limo? Or Himmler's silence, the sound of greasy plates soaking in a sink? I tried to stir myself free of a self-indulgent trauma trip.

No dice. I began to ruminate on the nature of cats and men.

• • •

A cat, if possessed of even an average IQ, learns early on what nastiness lurks in the heart of Man. On the contrary, Man knows jack-squat about cats – but believes he does, based on a few piddling observations. Unbeknownst to him, what the more wily animal permits him to see is nothing less than seamless mimicry.

The average domestic feline tips the Toledos at five to eight pounds. This is the approximate weight of a human newborn. If you think this is an accident, think again. When cradled against a chest a cat is warm, cuddly, and compliant. To Man, its mewling utterances are as cryptic as those of his own inarticulate progeny, and thus as winsome, distressing, exasperating, etc.

When purring, a cat sounds like a baby deep in slumber. When a cat looks up at Man with its big innocent eyes and wee chin, you have a decent replica of the looks, too. The similarities work subtly on the human mind, and they stir in people eleemosynary feelings. This is observed most strikingly in childless ladies of a certain age (hello, Fräulein Braun), who have had to straddle a hard ottoman, oohing and aahing counterfeit camaraderie, while a contemporary, riding a plush seven-foot long Madeleine davenport, suckles one of her burping brood. As an added bonus, cats, notwithstanding cases of illness or incontinent old age, one-up babies by not spilling vomit, urine, or worse on the people holding them.

Sure, *here kitty-kitty that's a nice kitty*, but Man does not see clearly through his anthropomorphic-colored glasses. He does not see the dirty work that goes into being a cat, particularly a homeless one in wartime.

Me, I know the score. I was in the hole ten-zip before my eyes even unstuck. I was born on the wrong side of the tracks, all right, and when I crossed the tracks I found the new side even wronger. Horror stories? This way, Bub – and sit down, this will take a while. I had my right ear slashed nearly clean off by a half-starved half-brother, all over a partially decomposed mouse. Hardly an hour passed that I was not robbed, beaten, or crapped on (literally). I scrapped in bloody turf wars, where the turf was a discount shoe store blown roofless by a Mustang P51-D. I witnessed countless murders, and even more countless rapes (with me on the ouch end more than once). There were even instances of cannibalism, carried out with dining etiquette that would have made a Sicilian blush.

And the worst of it is, these were all cat-on-cat atrocities.

Make no mistake, I fought my battles on mean streets. Without a father. And with a mother who really messed me up psychologically. My mother … Scheiße, it always comes back to Mutti. So be it. The armchair psychiatrists have to eat, too.

Most mother cats prepare alternate den sites for their young. I am not talking about lakeside summer villas, complete with gazebos, lawn chairs, and bosomy Swedish au pairs. I am talking about hide-outs from Tod, Herr Death himself. Numerous emergencies arise in the course of everyday feline life that make quick relocation necessary. The biggest threat is the appearance of an adult tom, because toms, when on the prowl for raised-tail action, will kill kittens not sired by themselves.

Now, I say *most* mother cats. Mutti was not like most. Whereas other mothers were wary of violent toms, Mutti actually *brought them home with her*. The first such occasion took place when I was perhaps a month old. It was a blustery winter evening in the south Berlin junkyard. My eleven brothers and I managed to ward off an icy end by napping in a furry heap in the small cardboard box that constituted our den.[17] I slept a lot then, not because I was lazy, but because I was young, and kittens need to sleep. One night I was dozing, probably dreaming of the food Mutti would never in a million trillion years see fit to share with me, when I awoke to a dreadful racket.

Next to the box loomed a huge tom, from my kitten's perspective as imposing as a saber-toothed tiger.

---

[17] By some Mendelian fluke, Mutti at one stage had pumped out 23 consecutive male kittens. These were only the siblings of which I knew.

He was thrashing his tremendous head back and forth, as if responding to the question, "Care for a neutering, sir?" Clenched between his long, sharp fangs was my brother Walli (or Berti – even they could not tell each other apart). The tom shook the kitten for a while, and then spit him out like a watermelon seed. Walli (or Berti) lay on the ground, bedraggled; right then, even if you had offered him his weight in fried pork for the feat, he would not have been able to point to his own tail. For the coup de grâce the tom bent down, and administered a quick bite to the back of the neck.

Now the hulking beast, with the breath he was snorting through wide noseholes visible in the frosty air, glared down into the cardboard box where we little ones remained, transfixed in fear. I think I can speak for all of us when I say that we felt our tender vittles wither up and retreat into our body cavities. Willi, bless him, was the first to run for it, and the rest of us followed suit. Before I left I got a good look at Mutti, who had just witnessed one of her own being snuffed out.

The heartless whore was licking herself in preparation for mating.

Willi and I stayed away for a week. (Our brothers returned the following morn.) To take our minds off the cold, we discussed, with teeth chattering like coins in a shaken piggy bank, the possibility of some rich kid finding and adopting a pair of emaciated kittens. Realistically we knew it was a no-go. We were flea-ridden junkyard cats, and the only response we could hope to get from a human was a punt in the ribs.

On our third or fourth night out, we encountered a wizened old tom living under a bridge by the Havel river. We were leery, naturally, but when he greeted us with a toothless yawn we knew infanticide was not on the menu. His gray head nodded us over to his modest den, a shallow pit encircled by rocks that kept the wind at bay.

He spoke with an accent I had never heard before, or since. "Good evenin', boys. Are ya lost? Can't foind yer Mutti?"

We looked down at our front paws.

"Yer Mutti's dead, eh?"

"We wish!" we cried in unison.

Willi added, "She doesn't give a scat about us!"

Then I recounted the fate that had befallen our brother.

The old tom sighed. "Boys, Oy bin around. Oy seen everyt'ing, eh? Oy's born on da Rock, near ta twenty years ago. Got moyself took in by a gen'rous sailor, Broyan Smit', may he rest in peace. Oy toored all da great cities. Rome, New York, St. John's. In Paris I even met Isadora Dongkin, two doys before da blue scarf t'ing. Here's whot Oy found: dis's a toff world. An' fer us cats it's gettin' ta be toffer. Lemme tells ya –" He stopped, and cocked his head to one side. "Listen, youse looks loike ya cud use a boite. An' Oy got me some squirrel here dat ain't com*plete*ly rancid yet."

The old tom scooped leftovers out from under a threadbare shawl. While we devoured the remains of a black squirrel (which was, in fact, completely rancid), he sat back and expounded upon what were obviously favorite themes. First he let loose on the contrasts between the Third Reich and its predecessor, the Weimar Republic. However, as politics did not jive us, Willi and I paid little attention. Likewise to the tom's riffs on Nostradamus, the Negro Jesse Owens's four golds at the '36 Olympics, and life on "da Rock" (whatever *that* was).

Then the old tom segued into the historical root of present-day feline problems.

"Dem Egyptian two-legs screwed us wit' dat dere *domesty-cation*. Sure dey was noice aboot it, even statued up a goddess in our image. Ever hear o' Bastis? But since dem pharoahs took us in we bin gettin' softer an' softer. Why not, eh? Lounge around all da day. Have fresh meat brung ta ya. Even get fanned by two-leg slaves when da sun's roastin' yer bott. But who controlled da breedin' after dat? Dem *two-legs*, dat's who! No more natural *see-lection*. Just Fifi an' Fluffy gettin' inbred over an' over til we's all weak an' pat'etic as poodles. Survoival o' da fittest? Survoival o' da *frailest*, more loike! So when we gots ta fend for ourselves, den whot? Up da *tree*, dat's whot! Moice an' rats an' dem rodential toypes, dey's *locky* da two-legs never took a loikin' to 'em! Dey bettered demselves t'roo evolution, eh? Bigger, stronger, meaner — even in moy own loifetime Oy seen da changes. Last mont' Oy hoiked out ta da countrysoide. Got to a pig farm near ta Oranienburg. Place was lousy wit' rats. Ya figgers Oy filled moy belly? Ya figgers wrong, boys. Dese were whot ya calls 'Norway rats,' which ain't even *from* Norway, dey's from *Asia*, fer Chroissakes!"

He shook his head in wonderment.

"Two points Oy wanna make in regards ta rats an' us. First, dem scaly-tails knowed all about da teamwork, which we cats ain't knowed since Cleopatra was a virgin. Second, dem rats was all monstered up like Russian lady shotputters. When Oy seen 'em dey was gat'ered round some grain bins. Da babies was gnawin' t'roo the wood walls, two inches t'ick, loike dey was potaty chips. Da adults was punchin' holes inta da bin. When Oy seen dis one sumbitch *headbott* his way in, dat's when Oy sez ta moyself ta get back ta Berlin. Oy seen enough, boys. Oy seen everyt'ing."

Willi and I gazed up at the old tom in awe. Bits of bad squirrel sat unchewed in our dry mouths. I swallowed, coughed for five minutes, and said, "Wow! I've never thought of *any* of that stuff before. What's your name, sir?"

"Name?" His laughter was benign, containing no hint of derision. "Names are fer *pets*, son. Oy ain't no pet. An' ta go by da filt'y coats yer wearin', youse two ain't, neit'er. Oy ain't got no name. But, if ya wants," he said with twinkle in his eye, "youse can call me ... Ecky."

"*Ecky.*" Willi and I murmured the name repeatedly, as if trying to wrest from the incantation some of the old tom's wisdom. Then, homage-like, I adopted his queer accent. "Mr. Ecky, dat was da perfectest t'ing Oy ever heard in moy loife! Oy feels like moy eyes bin opened a second toime!"

Willi chimed in, "An' Oy t'inks da same, sir!"

The old tom bowed his ancient head and smiled demurely. "T'anks, boys. But listen. Oy gots ta turn in now. Not cuz Oy'm lazy, but cuz old cats needs ta sleep. An' as ya sees fer yerself, moy accommodations ain't big enoff fer us all. Now youse can finish da squirrel, but den ya gots ta be off."

• • •

Himmler and I came upon a street that was teeming,

not with life but with life winding down. The hikers on the road were aged, faces like big angry peach pits, and all heading west. Accompanying them were morose, vermiculated-looking goats. These were put to work hauling wooden carts stacked high with table legs, bedrails, and broken chairs. *Lots* of broken chairs. Old people *love* broken chairs.

Himmler eased up on the gas pedal for a closer look at the ragged wayfarers. A few were sobbing quietly. Eventually curiosity got the better of him, and the SS leader pulled over and leaned on the klaxon button.

Two biddies, after setting the bicycles they had been pushing up on kickstands, came over. They sneered upon recognizing the driver. Between them they had about a dozen teeth, mostly metal. One clicked her clogs, and followed this not with a regular salute but by flipping us the bird.

By way of restraining himself, Himmler bit the inside of his cheek. He asked what it was they were fleeing. They answered by spraying the Nazi party with a torrent of waterfront language. Himmler took umbrage – though what he should have taken was an umbrella, since the nasty hags embodied the reason for the "say it, don't spray it" adage. In my driver's defense, I think anyone who had heard those grannies wetly mouthing off would also have shot them in the neck.[18]

We reached Nysa. A ghost town. Where were the Deustchesvolk? Where were the Poles? Most importantly, where was the food Frau Schultz was supposed to

---

[18] I could not, however, countenance what happened some ten miles later. Himmler, stopped at a red light, mowed down a squeegee kid. Hey, the spikey-haired youngster was only trying to make a Mark. And the windshield did look a lot better.

have prepared especially for me? Scheiße! Fräulein Braun had forgotten to pack it!

When we turned onto the main street Himmler suddenly slammed on the brakes. I knocked my head on the glove box. After shaking out the cobwebs I hopped up to the dashboard. There, not fifty feet before us, I saw a platoon of Yanks standing in their blunt-toed combat boots.

Himmler checked in the rearview mirror and cried, "Gottdamn it!" I jumped down onto the seat, then up onto the headrest, and looked out behind us. A US Army jeep was speeding towards us. Himmler turned off the ignition and slumped forward, his forehead pressed against the wheel.

The gutless quitter.

As for me, I had not come this far to be locked away and left to rot in a military prison, Gavrilo Princip-style, by some ten-pin bowling, Perry Como-listening, comic book lip-reading, New World cretin. I yanked my armband off and stuffed it under the seat. When Himmler saw that, the copycat copied the cat. Then, realizing that his uniform was a giveaway, he grabbed Kempka's velvet smoking jacket from the back seat. I helped the SS klutz stick his spindly arms into the sleeves. He found a spare burgundy ascot and tied it about his pencil neck.

A soldier, with an M1 Garand rifle slung manfully over his broad left shoulder, approached the driver's side of the limo. He flashed an all-American grin: thick, white, non-metallic teeth, and though I did not count I was sure there were thirty-two of them. "Good afternoon, sir," he boomed cheerfully, after motioning for Himmler to roll down the window. He sported MacArthur shades that reflected, as in a funhouse mirror, the SS leader's swirling face. "I'm Sergeant Buzz Plunkett of the US Army." He bent back at the waist to take in the full length of the Mercedes. "Ni-i-ice wheels."

Himmler's head bobbed, in the inane "oh-yes-I-suppose-so-if-you-say-so" manner.

Now the soldier leaned forward and placed his forearms nonchalantly across the roof of the limo. Completely relaxed. He could have been a suburbanite talking over the backyard fence with his neighbor, taking a breather from pushing around the old lawn mower to debate Eintracht Frankfurt's chances against Hertha Berlin's in the upcoming Bundesliga match. "Mind answerin' a few questions, sir?"

Himmler contemplated the tip of his nose for moment. "Nein."

"Oh! You're German. That's odd. I'll tell ya why. Because most of your gang beelined west a while ago. What business do you have in these parts, sir?"

Himmler blinked like Fräulein Braun's reading lamp when the maid vacuumed. "I'm a ... *chauffeur.*"

"Uh-huh. And what's your name, sir?"

"Hein-" I faked a series of violent sneezes; Himmler caught on. "Erich Kempka."

"Well, Mr. Kempka, d'ya have any objections to me sneakin' a peekaboo at your driver's license?"

Himmler twisted around to pull out his wallet – his *own* wallet! Once again I saved the day when I pawthumped the glove box. It fell open, slack-jawed, like my buddy in the driver's seat.

"Smart cat," the Yank said.

Himmler tried to affect Kempka's rakish smile as the soldier compared the photograph of the lady's man to the slightly-built ex-chicken farmer trembling in the limo. Satisfied (!), the soldier handed back the license.

"Are you the owner of this vehicle, Mr. Kempka?"

Himmler looked over at me. I shook my head. "Nein," he said.

"May I see the registration, please?"

The SS leader reached into the glove box and pulled out the papers.

The soldier removed his shades, slipped them into his coat pocket, and pored over the document. "Pardon me, sir. I can't make out the letters in this flowery olden times script. Does that say Adolf ... *Nitler?*"

Himmler's lips made an O as he exhaled anxiously. He thrust his hand over his left breast to muffle the beating, à la Poe's tell-tale heart character. "Ja. Adolf Nitler."

"So, if I got this right, sir. You *work* for Mr. Nitler?"

The blinks-per-second now approached the rate of a silent film harlot's trying to get a rise out of Rudi Valentino. "Ja. Ja, ja. Ja!"

"Uh-huh." The soldier frowned thoughtfully, as if what he were about to say caused him mild indigestion. "I don't want to offend you, sir. But, well, you understand, I *have* to ask. Are you, or Mr." – he sneaked another peekaboo at the papers – "Nitler, in any way affiliated with the Nazi party?"

Himmler looked out the windshield, then back at his interrogator. "Nein."

The soldier's grin returned. "That's good. That's *real* good, because we got orders to arrest Nazis on sight." He looked past Himmler and gave me the once-over, twice. "Say, what's the cat's name?"

The question was one too many, and had an unwholesome effect upon Himmler. His head lolled back. He was scrutinizing the limo's ceiling light when he howled, "*Heinrich Himmler!*"

The entire platoon stopped to look over. Everything went quiet, earholes gasping for oxygen like at a poetry reading when the poet sips water between stanzas to stifle his cottonmouth. The soldier stared at us deadpan, looking like the never-painted son of the gruesome "American Gothic" twosome.

Then he giggled, before breaking out in laughter. "Heinrich *Himmler!* Ha! The cat's called Heinrich *Himmler!* That's hilarious! I thought you Jerries weren't big on gags, but *that's* funny! Heinrich *Himmler*, ha ha ha!" The soldier moseyed on off to share the jocularity with the other doughboys.

Himmler shut his eyes tight, and clasped his hands together in a silent prayer.

The soldier returned, more collected. "Well, thanks for the belly laugh, Mr. Kempka. The fellas liked that one. So, I guess that's about all, then. Sorry to take up your time. You have a good one, okay?"

Himmler mopped his brow with the cuff of the smoking jacket, and turned the key in the ignition. The limo, like an inexpert shoplifter who cannot believe the gullible deli clerk fell for the old "Oops, I forgot that kielbasa was in my pocket!" line, lurched and rolled into motion, shaky but relieved.

Needless to say, not a word of thanks was directed my way.

• • •

After the close call with the Yanks, Himmler, heedful of falling into another trap, navigated cagily, a merchant ship's captain wary of hostile fleets. He stopped every half mile or so to peer into his binoculars at what sailed on the waters ahead. A stony stare had darkened his pasty face. His dull brown eyes, always beady behind the wire-framed specs, threw less light than usual – a paradox, in that the stillness in his eyes somehow reflected hysterical calculations within. I thought of a giant old turtle I had once seen, assailed on the mossy banks of a pond by a pair of yip-yapping dogs, and of the impassive expression on its pitiable-yet-proud Indian chief puss – just before a mean chomp, catapulted by a startlingly long piston-swift neck, claimed a paw.

We reached a gloomy forest, where firs and spruces crackled and moaned under the bitter wind like arthritic reindeer in a Santa Claus parade. After relieving ourselves on a massive stump (pen-knife engraved with "Karl ♥ Ilse"), we camouflaged the limo in branches. Himmler settled into the back seat, pulled his leather top-coat over himself, and fell asleep. In the fetal position (*big* surprise). I caught forty winks up front.

It was a whisker-chiller of a night, according to the dashboard thermometer minus 40 – and do not ask if it was Celsius or Fahrenheit, it was *cold* is all I know. So harsh was it that my footpads, had one of the Goebbels brats tossed me into the air right then, would on landing have broken off like a leper's toes. We did not avail ourselves of the heater, for that would have meant leaving the motor on, wasting fuel, and perhaps drawing attention to our hideout. What is more, my stomach was as empty as Göring's bravado, and Himmler, beset by nightmares, woke me several times with tiny helium screams. I longed for the warmth and security of Hitler's darling size six feet.

• • •

At dawn, groggy as zoo gorillas, we embarked for Auschwitz. The sun was a pallid 20-watter set against a vast gray ceiling. We kept the windows rolled down, hoping the air would invigorate us. For once, Fate knocked its crowbar on someone else's kneecap, and we skirted any more nail-biters with Uncle Sam's goons. Not a soul appeared on the road for hours. I got down on the floorboard, by the heating duct, and curled up to sleep.

Shortly before arriving at our destination, an acrid stench slapped our faces like a furious pimp. I climbed up onto the seat and searched without for the source (Himmler, unlike Göring, was not given to bouts of noxious flatulence). Above us, rising from the stacks of a red brick building, I saw towering columns of haughty black smoke. In the sky they converged, and flowed together like a swarm of locusts heading for the harvest.

We rolled up our windows faster than Buster Keaton on beanies. I buried my snout in my shoulder. Himmler scrunched his eyes and pinched his nose-holes like a gawky kid stepping off the high board. Soon we grew as teary as Goldi reading the final sentence of the romance novel, "A Milkmaid in Love."[19] The unbearable fetor – what was it, a million old boots, filled with rubber bands and rotten bacon, doused in petrol, and set afire? – was like nothing I

---

[19] "And after that gentle kiss from Count von Schuschnigg, Monika – the future Countess von Schuschnigg – would never again walk into her degenerate step-father's barn, pull up her dress, plop onto the wooden stool, and coarsen her fair hands on the udders of a grunting cow."

had ever encountered before.[20] I held my breath for dear life, in even more agony than the time I had tripped on bad catnip and found myself in a beveling outhouse, dancing the mazurka with three trollops of my own excrement.

The windshield had been mugged and befouled. The origins of the gritty film I did not then know (and even now shudder to think about). My co-Nazi cussed when, after fiddling with several knobs, no saving fluid was forthcoming from the wiper tank. He shifted into neutral, stepped out of the limo still pinching his noseholes, and with his free hand buffed the grime out with Kempka's soon-to-be-ruined ascot.

Twenty minutes later Himmler swung into the Auschwitz parking lot, backed into a reserved spot, and killed the engine. We hiked our armbands back on in a kind of shameful silence, as if we had insulted their honor by stuffing them away like a boy with his mother's girdle catalogue when the bathroom door unexpectedly swung open. Himmler found his officer's cap and put it on, taking care to fasten the silver braided cord where his chin, if he had one, would be.

We tramped along a snowy path. Up ahead, a bomb-shriveled train station struggled to maintain the loosening mask of pre-shelling vitality. About

---

[20] The only incident which even began to approach this level of stink occurred in the bunker in early April. Der Führer, in wild-eyed desperation, ordered Frau Schultz to turn over her kitchen (under Speer's slow but careful supervision) to the assembly line preparation of his latest and greatest "secret weapon" – Frau Göring's strudel. Let the record show that Operation Apfelstrudel, like the Nazi plans to develop an atomic bomb, never got off the ground. By that stage of the war even the resourceful Speer could not scrounge up enough flour and raisins for the assigned task.

fifty SS guards were huddled by the track, some tugging at the leashes of barking Alsatians, others puffing cancer sticks. All of their heads drooped beneath the weight of their steel helmets. No one seemed put off by the stench.

As we neared I heard the growing rumble of a train, as well as the guards passing word along that their skipper had arrived. They shushed the dogs, stamped out their Luckies, and stood at attention. When we got close enough they clicked their heels and gave sieg heils – by rote, without the rah-rah of the bunker guards.

There were other signs that did not bode well for our side in the conflict. One, the guards' uniforms were stained with soot, frayed at the edges, and a size too big. Two, so were their teeth. Three, their rusty rifles hung off their shoulders *from fricken ropes*. Now compare and contrast with the smartly-tailored, dazzlingly white-toothed Sergeant Buzz Plunkett of the US Army, whose well-oiled Garand had hung proudly from a new leather strap.

A whistle sounded. From the station door a dark-haired man, handsome in a street corner Romeo way, stepped briskly out, and fitted a monocle over his left eye. He looked boss in his stylishly tight-fitting officer's uniform (though without a cap). In his right hand he held a white conductor's baton. Finding his mark, a white-painted 'X' on the pavement, he stopped, and raised the baton high over his head. On cue, the tinny loudspeakers fixed under the roof of the platform crepitated to life, and two seconds of record scratch gave way to the opening strains of "The Marriage of Figaro."

This was Doctor Josef Mengele, AKA the Angel of Death.[21]

He was slim. And I pegged him at 5'6", since he was about half a foot taller than the jutting forefinger of the park ride cardboard figure, grinning like a fool next to him. The bulb-nosed clown extended its left arm out, under which hung a sign from two small chains bearing the words: "If you are too sick to work in the quarry, or pregnant, or don't come up to my finger (5 feet), YOU MUST GO LEFT!"

Also distinguishing Mengele from the garden variety Nazi were the white kid gloves he wore. Over the cacophony of the train's arrival, he waved his arms about like Toscanini trying to impress a busty knockout he had spotted in the tenth row. It was as if he were conducting not a Mozart libretto, but something with repeated cannon blasts. Even in that obscurant din, I could hear the sharp *wheet* of his wand slicing the air. Even with the funky depravity lashing at my noseholes like stink-whips, I could detect the ethereal cologne bedewed over him. In short, the doctor looked, acted, and smelled like a gentleman, one who could plunk felicitous quotations into any conversation.

The wheels of the cattle wagons screeched to a halt, and the locomotive exhaled the sibilance of a sighing steel snake. Himmler and I ignored the crew climbing

---

[21] Doctor Mengele's nickname was self-applied, after many attempts to find the right fit. Some of the previous handles: The Günzburg Kid. The King of Sting. The Queen of Mean. The Prince of Wince. The Duke of Puke. The Deacon of Doom. The Priest of Pain. The Archbishop of Canterbury. The Doc of Shock. The Vicious Physician. The "Put That Midget There In The Frigidaire" Operator. The Twin Reaper. The Eye Dye Guy. The Evil Rectum of Collect 'em, Infect'em, and Disect 'em.

down from the caboose onto the platform. We watched Mengele, jitter-bugging like a mental patient warding off hornets. As the color commentators would have it, he was giving a hundred and ten percent, perfectly lip-synching the words, swivelling his hips, and kicking his legs high as a Busby Berkely chorus girl. His head jerked up and down, so that a great chunk of his silky hair would fall forward over his eyes, and then take its place again on the back of his head, where it wiggled a bit until the measure changed again, and the process began anew.

The music faded out. Mengele – as if a goateed hypnotist had right before his eyes snapped his fingers three times – broke free of the trance. The guards clapped. The doctor bowed. Someone handed him his hat. After quickly running a comb through his hair, he put it on, leaving the silver chinstrap coiled up on the shiny black bill, against the band. Then he spotted Himmler, and walked over to us.

The three of us exchanged sieg heils. Mengele did not (à la Goebbels, "von" Ribbentrop, and Bormann) point and cry, "Lookit the cat! Lookit the cat! Someone taught it the salute!"[22] He removed the

---

[22] No one had "taught" me. I had taken up the salute on my second or third day in the bunker. I was watching Hitler late one evening in the anteroom, pulling futilely on Blondi's right front paw. "Come on, girl," he pleaded. "It's easy! Like this. 'Sieg heil!' See? 'Sieg heil!' You can do it, girl. Even Bormann can do it … sort of." Blondi's response would have been sufficient only if the command had been, "Stick your tongue way out and look really, really stupid." (Could she do any tricks? Just one: if you poked her in the eye, she winked.) I thereupon executed a perfect sieg heil. Hitler looked over at me, stunned. I repeated the salute a few times, even knocking the ankles of my hind legs together to make the click (which really hurt – not that I let on). Alas, rather than promote me to Official Pet of the Nazi Party, Hitler merely let go of the dog foot, rose in disgust, and went to see if Göring had not gobbled up all the chili yet.

glove on his right hand, and, in a manner reminiscent of a buttery Baroness anticipating a knuckle smooch, held it by the finger-tips of his left. With great formality, he said, "Herr Reich Leader of the SS, a pleasure to see you again!"

Himmler, a kalter fisch if ever there was one, shook the hand warmly. "Come now, Doctor! How long have we known each other? I'm H2 to my friends."

Mengele released Himmler's mitt and enthused, "As you wish, H2. And you in turn shall do me the honor of calling me 'The Angel of Death.'"

Himmler's left eyebrow shot up. "What happened to 'The Deacon of Doom?'"

"Oh." Mengele blushed. "I got a cease and desist on that one. From Franzi Stangl, over in Treblinka."

"No kidding? Why would Franzi –"

"It's not important," Mengele broke in, dismissing the subject with a flick of his wrist.

"*You* brought it up! Come on, don't be a tease!"

Mengele, realizing he was stuck, puffed his cheeks up in resignation, and let the air slowly seep out. "Well, it goes back to the time Stangl and I debated death chamber poisons. Remember? At the Wannsee meeting?"

"Vaguely."

"He was pushing carbon monoxide. Very passé. *I* wanted to leap into the twentieth century with hydrogen cyanide pellets. Of course, when the annual reports came out, and Team Auschwitz was leading the league, poor Stangl wound up with egg on his face. But rather than do something constructive about it, he set out to humiliate me. You know how those Treblinka guys are."

"What'd he do?"

"He filed a copyright suit. Claimed that my 'Deacon

of Doom' infringed on his 'Doomsday Dealer.'" Smiling acidly, Mengele kicked a stone. "And the judge agreed."

"'Doomsday Dealer?' I thought Franzi was 'The Real Deal.'"

"You're mixing him up with the old boxer," Mengele said. "Hector 'The Real Deal' Stangl. No relation."

Himmler slapped his forehead. "Ja, the middleweight. Glass jaw. I lost a bundle on one of his fights. Must've been ten years ago. I wonder what that bum's up to now."

"Pumping gas somewhere, no doubt," Mengele opined, with palpable boredom. He bent to stroke my ears. Then, with hands as slim and persnickety as a Parisian sculptor's butt, he goosed mc one. "Male, I see. What's his name?"

"How should I know?"

"Nice fur. Someone's been brushing him. I liked the sieg heil bit. You pick him up hitch-hiking?" Mengele kidded.

"Nein," replied Himmler, who got jokes as readily as Eskimos got sunburns. "He's der Führer's."

"Ja? I thought Maximum Leader was a dog man?"

"Eva made him. Just between you and me, that little lady's getting too big for her britches."

Mengele gave a worldy laugh. "'I know the disposition of women: when you will, they won't; and when you won't, they set their hearts upon you of their own inclination.'" (I knew he could quote!)

"Huh?"

"Terence said that."

"The Mauthausen janitor?" Himmler snorted. "Figures."

Mengele turned his attention back to me. "You know,

I feel as if I've met this cat before. Was he around when I dropped by last month to put that maid to sleep?"

"Not sure." Himmler brightened. "But you should check out the new maid, Angel of Death." The SS leader gave a wolf whistle. "I may take Fräulein Müller out for a little test drive myself. That is, if that playboy chauffeur hasn't already put his, uh ... gearshift into ... her thing, the doodad next to the carburetor ... it sort of looks like a – "

"Speaking of which," Mengele cut in, mercy-killing the deformed metaphor, "how was the ride in from Berlin?"

Himmler did the torpid turtle face again. "Ja."

The doctor continued stroking me. "I just know I've seen this cat somewhere."

The train conductor joined us. "Doctor, we're ready for you."

Mengele pulled out a watch-fob out and glanced at it. "Let's rock and roll."

The subsequent procedure struck me as unusual, to say the least. I chalked it up to local custom, figuring that it was something I understood imperfectly because they did things differently here from the big city. For, as I have already stated (and it is true!), until that time I knew *nothing* of the Nazi machinations with respect to what would later come to be known as the Final Solution.

Mengele marched to the very first wagon in the convoy. Trailing him was a straggly line of guards, each with a truncheon in hand. One of the guards jumped onto a step and unbolted a lock. Then, throwing his full weight into the effort, he slid the door open. He hopped back down and shouted, "Raus!"

Nothing stirred from within the darkened space. It required much yelling, and the kettledrumming of ten truncheons on the outside of the wagon, to allow us a glimpse of the first passengers. A woman, barefoot and very underdressed for a winter day, appeared squinting at the light. Pressed to her bosom and wrapped in rags was a baby, and holding her hand was a boy of about three. She wrenched the youngster aloft, risking shoulder dislocation by stretching his arm out like that. Descending uncertainly to the step, and then to the ground, she stumbled and nearly sent all of them sprawling.

A guard passed Mengele a white megaphone. He pressed it to his lips, and said, "Willkommen to Auschwitz! My name is Doctor Mengele! Those of you with jewelry or other valuables please deposit them in the wheel barrow nearest your wagon!"

The baby cried, and the boy released his mother's hand and covered both earholes. The megaphone, clearly, was a prop, for Mengele stood less than three feet from the trio.

Notwithstanding the aural pain he was inflicting, the doctor's trainside manner proved impeccable. "Now, madam," he said, conversationally, "you will go to the right, and your children to the left. A shower, hot meal, and warm bed await you all!"

The woman, rather than be satisfied with this – to my way of thinking, at least – hospitable offer, grew visibly consternated. "No! I must be with my children!"

Mengele smiled and spoke slowly, as might a kind maître d' when explaining escargot to Texan tourists. "Very well, madam. As you wish. At Camp Auschwitz we have two dictums: Arbeit Macht Frei, and The

Customer is Always Right. Guard, escort this woman and her children to the left."

And on it went. Many women were similarly disinclined to be separated from their offspring, and Mengele cheerfully obliged them. Several of the male passengers had long, unkempt beards and curious sidelocks. At no cost, they were shorn of their facial hair right there on the platform. The SS guards seemed to have misplaced their scissors, so they made do with infantry bayonets. Even so, the amateur barbers conducted themselves competently, with only a few of the hirsute passengers suffering serious lacerations.

In compliance with the cardboard clown's directive, the weak, pregnant, and short were sent to the left, with the exception (the rationale behind which escaped me) of twins, midgets, and Gypsies. Heading to the right as well were two plucky imps who stood next to the clown on tippytoes. There was also a game, which I fairly enjoyed, played with able-bodied adults, for even when they did "come up to my finger" a pass to the right was not a given. The doctor, twirling his baton, would hum a few bars of a composition through the megaphone and then say, "Name that tune!" If the passenger answered incorrectly, he went to the left. For the time I kept score, I scored 16 out of 17 (Strauss's "Der Rosenkavalier" threw me, for some reason). One man who guessed wrong – he thought "Eine Kleine Nacht Musik" was "Ain't She Sweet" – became so distraught at being told to go left that he began tearing out his hair. But the doctor, even as two guards dragged off the sore loser, never stopped smiling.

When the passengers were all sorted out, it was just after noon. After a quick lunch in the Auschwitz mess hall (sausages, which tasted a bit... *strange*), Mengele invited us on a tour of the compound. We walked first to his laboratory building. Inside, he opened the door to a room, and there we saw eight people standing on their heads. "Oh," Mengele said, flustered. "I'd forgotten this was still here."

Some of the subjects opened their eyes; none spoke. An iron contraption held them aloft. I did not see how they could get down on their own, I mean for toilet purposes. I supposed that a lab assistant came by every few minutes to monitor such things.

When Himmler asked about the experiment, Mengele said, "It's kind of technical, H2. A blood circulation thing. Actually, I've got cooler stuff down the hall."

It was in this second room that I put two and two together, and the answer was, "Oh man, this is some sick scheiße!"

The first thing to catch my eye were the eyeballs. Hundreds of them, in little cases on the walls, pinned like exotic moths in a natural museum, and arranged in such a way as to suggest the colors of the spectrum – indigo and violet on one side, passing to red, orange, and yellow on the other.

"The results of my methylene dye research."

Himmler looked queasy. "These scientific, uh, thingamajigs are way over my head."

Mengele, having no doubt grown accustomed to this sort of declination, took it in stride. "Right. But let me show you what else I'm cooking up."

We moseyed on over to a large steel cabinet, where Mengele unlocked and flung open the doors. Scores of specimen jars sat on the shelves, and the doctor proceeded to take them out one at a time. He provided a running commentary on the contents of each jar, although I must admit I recall none of what was said. I was too busy staring at what he was holding in his hands. Floating in formaldehyde solutions, in jar after jar, were such objects as hearts, severed fingers, and twin babies' heads.

Then Mengele came to one he called his "all-time favorite." He untwisted the cap, and, like a man angling for the last pickle, fished out the dripping penis of a midget (testes attached). This was too much. Himmler and I did synchronized pirouettes, crouched, and expelled "sausage" bits onto the floor.

After composing ourselves, we turned again to face Mengele. The quack was still holding the midget bits, squishing them around like a Chinaman with Ben Wa balls, and looking puzzled by our reaction. "Was the sausage undercooked?"

"Ja," Himmler said, wiping his mouth on his sleeve. "Let's go shoot the cook in the neck."

"Now? But I've still got a lot of other –"

"Now!"

. . .

After attending to the execution of the cook, the three of us went for a stroll outdoors. It was getting colder as the sun began to set. The pestilential odor, somehow, had worsened. Mengele, remarking that diphtheria and scarlet fever were reaching epidemic proportions, withdrew from his pocket two surgical masks; in this way, Himmler and he were provided with a shield against germs, while I, naturally, was left to fend for myself. I noticed that a tip-truck was parked next to the crematoria, and that the chimneys were emitting fresh smoke. I thought it a small grace note that at least we were not there in summer.

Mengele, with hands clasped behind his back, spoke wistfully. "I'm going to be sorry to leave this place. I mean, it's been tough slogging lately, especially after the gas chambers got bombed a couple months ago. Boy, we really scrambled to get some new ones up! Still, Auschwitz has been a really positive experience for me. It's as if I went back to high school, and was able to re-live those blissful days. And now I'm graduating. To what, I don't know."

Himmler, who I am sure spent *his* high school days reaching around to remove the "kick me" signs pinned to his backside, asked Mengele what his plans were when the time came to close up shop.

Mengele stopped walking, and with a big grin pulled out a passport from his vest pocket. He handed it to Himmler, who read it and handed it back.

"Adolf Fuddrucker? Where'd you come up with *that* alias?"

"Adolf is self-explanatory. And Herr Fuddrucker was my chemistry teacher at Bismarck High."

"Bismarck High? Really? I went to Kaiser Wilhelm! We *hated* you guys!"

We resumed our tour of the grounds, passing first a lookout tower, where an armed guard stood watch, and then a barracks enclosed in a barbed wire fence. I was able to make out several figures outside the row of ram-shackle buildings, shambling in the cold glow of white spotlights. They were remnants of humanity, lingering like crippled souls in a smelly purgatory: blank eyes staring out of hollowed sockets, concave bellies, twist-ed elbows and knees protruding through dirty striped pajamas, all of them as skinny as supermodels. It was here that I heard, for the first time, the word "Jews."

"Jews," said Himmler, looking over for a moment.

"Ja, no kidding," Mengele said.

Suddenly, in the midst of this degradation, I heard something that shocked me even further: a meow. I glanced over, and right there, not ten feet away, I saw a cat, just inside the fence, waving a paw frantically in my direction.

Willi!

I ran to my brother. (Mengele and Himmler, paying no notice to my absence, continued their leisurely pace.) "Willi, what in hell are you doing in there!" I tried to stick a paw through the fence, and for my effort was zapped.

"It's electrified," he said, giving a tubercular cough. To my amazement, he appeared to be even more sickly and malnourished than when I had last seen him! "And what am *I* doing in here?" he continued. "What in hell are *you* doing wearing a Nazi armband, Erwin?"

"Actually, it's Tutti now. Tutti Hitler. But listen, Willi, how did –"

"Actually, it's Shlomo now."

"Shlomo?"

"Shlomo Friedman."

Then he spoke of the heartbreaking events which had led him to this cesspool of despair.

After leaving Berlin, Willi headed east, riding freight trains, getting off at stops here and there to see if the locale offered any promise. When it did not, he would hop aboard and stow away on the next train. Eventually he came to Krakow, and there was taken in by a Jewish boy he encountered one night, both of them searching for food in a razed market. The boy took him home to his family's hiding spot, a cellar on the outskirts of town. Despite the lack of sunlight (they only went out at night), the conditions were a slight improvement over what Willi had had with me back in Berlin, so he stayed on. He had meat (no ham, though), and milk (powdered), and in time put on some weight – a welcome turn of events that, all in all, more than offset the excruciating torture he had endured at the bris.

The family consisted of a married couple and their two adolescent sons. One spent all his time with his pencil and diary; but the other, the one who had found Willi, coddled my brother, even sneaking him portions of his own food.

One day the storm troopers kicked in the attic door. Finding nothing there, they left empty-handed. A week later, however, they remembered that they had not checked the cellar. Now they hauled away the whole family. My brother hid behind the Jew's harp, but the younger boy, his benefactor, exclaimed, "Hey! Let's bring Shlomo, too."

"So here I am, Brother. Oy vey! Starving, circumcised, and with my own fricken number." He held up his left fore leg and showed me the seven digits engraved there.

"This is madness," I said, at a loss for a more grandiloquent phrase.

"I'll say," he agreed, coughing again. "Look at me. Blue in the face, hacking my guts out like a fat chainsmoker. I can't sleep. I haven't had a decent meal since … Wait a minute. Did you say Tutti *Hitler?*"

While he looked on in astonishment, I told him my own story.

When I finished, he asked, "So, you'll help me?"

"Of course. At least, if – I'm here with Himmler, and, uh –"

"*Heinrich* Himmler? Head honcho of the SS?"

"We call him H2. He owes me. I saved his popo on the way here."

We were joined then by Himmler and Mengele, who had circled back on the path. My weary brain raced to formulate a plan. How I wished I could have taken a nap right then! Alas, everything unravelled like a cheap Albanian sweater.

Mengele picked up on the resemblance. "Mein Gott, they could be twins!" he gushed. "I think they *are* twins! I've always wanted to extend my research to quadrupeds!"

"Twin cats?" Himmler said, without much interest.

"Of course! Just look at them! And the rapport they have! I must have that cat, H2!"

"I don't know," Himmler said. "Eva would be pretty teed off."

"This one has a mole under the left eye, and ... *so does this one!* And the tails! Each has a black mark on the tip of his tail! And see how yours stays by the fence, as if he's just found his long lost brother!"

"They *do* seem awful friendly."

"*Please* let me have him! I have a special experiment in mind, so fiendishly cruel that even *I* think it too beastly to try on human twins!"

"That's all well and good, Angel of Death, but there's still Eva to consider." Then Himmler closed his eyes. I could sense that he was waffling. "On the other hand, I *do* know for a fact that der Führer hates this cat."

On that ominous note, I decided that my life should not be left in the feckless hands of a near-sighted ex-chicken farmer. Willi was screwed. That was regrettable, but there was no good reason for me to down with him.

Acting quickly, I sent my paw flying through a gap in the barbed wire and scratched Willi in the eye. This, I hoped, would prove that no familial connection existed between us.

Next, I walked over to my Nazi escort. Shamelessly, and right in front of my brother's one open eye, I slutted it up all over Himmler's leg, rubbing and purring and gazing up at him with all the fake love and devotion I could muster.

"Ach," Himmler said, at last. "Forget it. Eva would have conniption."

"Well," Mengele shrugged, "I guess that's that. Let's go back to my office and get those relocation papers signed."

Behind us, Willi bawled, like a naked baby left alone in the woods as the winter night closed in.

Meat

MRUMM, MRUMM, MRUMM, MRUMM.

The limousine, a rolling choir of special class kids, was humming an inane one-note ditty. Under the brass-knuckled sky, bruised with clouds, leafless trees zipped past, blurred and swaying as in a catnip hallucination. Next to me sat Madame Tussaud's "Himmler."

There were no heart-stopping road checks; no stragglers for my driver to shoot in the neck; no amorous lady hitch-hitchers packing doobies in the back pockets of their cut-off dungarees. There was only time, pitiless and immovable, squatting on my chest like a brute with Limburger breath, barking, "You best mull over what you done, buddy boy!"

I tried to lose myself in a nap, but for the first time in my life instant slumber proved elusive. With no escape, and alone with my thoughts, the guilt pummelled me. For the duration of the nineteen hour ride, I beat myself up like a masochist on his birthday.

After the war hypocrisy, a resilient weed among ruins and shattered dreams, sprouted everywhere. In the summer of '45, underground resistance "heroes" came out of the woodwork like termites shaken from a waking pirate's peg-leg. Suddenly everyone had a Jew in the attic, a case of Old Milwaukee in the kitchen, and an Acme Assassinate-der-Führer Kit™ in the closet. What a bunch of … Ach, never mind.

Those of us who survived the war did so by compromising our consciences in a thousand little ways. A bit of lying here, some filched rations there, and some turned backs on brothers in order to save our own furry popos. I grant that I sound like one of those roly-poly burgomeisters, bullscheißing a denazification committee as the sweat pours out of his earholes. I am no hero, but am I such a villain? Consider the risks in trying to spring Willi from the camp. Would I, the brother of a Jewish cat, have been exterminated? Or "merely" experimented upon? You might smugly counter, as you read this memoir in the comfort of your reclining armchair, with your slippered feet propped up just so by the crackling fireplace, that Himmler would not have allowed the Angel of Death to harm Hitler's pet. There is the rub – I was *Fräulein Braun's* pet! As such, should I have gone double or nothing for Willi's sake? What if we *had* gotten away? We would have been together again, sure, but hungry and homeless. It was a game of snakes and ladders, and a single roll of the dice could see me riding that slippery legless lizard all the way back to square one.

What was certain was that acknowledging kinship with Willi would have jeopardized the sweet deal I had going, and to what end? There was no chance Himmler, aware of the contempt in which I was then held by der Führer, would have taken Willi back to Berlin with us; knowing the big guy barely tolerated me, he was not about to usher another cat into the bunker mix. And, as ashamed as I am to admit it, I did not want my brother there, because that would have meant one more rival for Hitler's affection, and therefore for meat.

There. I said it. I chose meat over my brother, because to choose otherwise was to deny my own nature. A cat without meat is not a cat; he is a rabbit with claws. And while even the lowest alley cat enjoys the possibility of securing meat, let me tell you that it is no picnic obtaining food that happens to have a pulse. Food that is terrified of you. Food that hears your stomach growling at a hundred paces, and that upon your approach runs faster than it has ever run before. Food that, if cornered, will *fight back*, because it is as hellbent on its sorry survival as you are on yours.[23]

In the limo, after the episode at the fence, I took inventory of my physique. I had grown a belly. My coat, thanks to a few bucket baths from the maid, was thick and glossy, and no longer moonlighted as a flea and louse bed and breakfast.[24] Finally, there was the armband on my leg that trumpeted for all the world to hear: "Make way, chumps! Nazi pet coming through!" These external changes were a still-wet layer of paint that scantily covered my crumbling tenement of a life. Was this new me really *me?* Was *I* a Nazi? What did it mean, to be a Nazi pet? I could not answer, but I decided that, whatever I had become, it was better than what I had until recently been: a mangy loser of a dope fiend.

However well off I was in comparison to my former

[23] Near the end of the war, conditions on the street had deteriorated to such an extent that more than a few of my feline acquaintances – a varied cast that included old-timers, 'nip addicts, and lamers – had gone veggie. Cripes, some had even taken to proselytizing on the health benefits of grass, or waxing poetic on the need to respect the "intrinsic dignity" of our fellow mammals. As fricken if! Eating our fellow mammals was what made us mammals, at least respectable ones. And I had no intention of transforming myself, à la the bamboo-sucking panda, into a vegetarian.

[24] By this time, I had licked out the Auschwitz ashes that had fallen onto me like dandruff from Hephaestus's head. Blondi, to carry through with the Greek imagery, would have worn that dirt until Zephyr blew it off.

straits, I realized that my newfound security hung by a tenuous thread. Blipping across my radar screen were the Allies and their superior firepower, Frau Schultz and her soup ladle, Göring and his Luger, and, of course, that *dog*, looming like a big stupid hairy mountain between Hitler and me. As cold-blooded as it sounds, I did not need plopped in my path one more obstacle. And that was what Willi, in my mind's eye stuck forever behind barbed wire, represented.

· · ·

We returned just before dawn. Himmler, using more elbow grease than Fräulein Braun had ever required, wrenched open the trapdoor and let me into the bunker. He went to get a cup of phony coffee at the all-night diner around the corner. Did he inquire as to whether I might desire some cream for to quench my thirst? I assure you he did not.

I found the door to Hitler and Fräulein Braun's room closed. To judge by the stale cigarette smoke (a recent habit taken up by der Führer) that wafted out from under the door, they had retired only recently. A few feet away, on the hallway floor, Blondi, "on guard" against assassins, was sprawled out and dead to the world. Her tongue was out, fat and unfurled, like a cow's at the butcher shop. Her saliva collected into a wading pool on the linoleum. Johnny Weismuller could have managed a few freestyle strokes in that puddle.

In the rest of the Four Star, Goebbels was the only one up. His bedroom door was ajar, and for a while I watched him, hunched over in his lower bunk. A pencil, pad, and flashlight aided him as he fine-tuned a radio

speech. Intermittently he mouthed a passage, with ges-
ticulating flourishes, and then shook his head in self-
reproach. Then he would put an eraser to work, brush
the detritus off the page, and concentrate on a more
inspiring (that is, more deceitful) phrasing. Once, he
angrily jabbed the pencil into the mattress above him;
there, Bormann was snoring like an actor hamming it up
in a community theater comedy.

Ham? I went for a stroll into the other half of the
bunker, hoping that Kempka or the maid might be
around to make with some chow.

The B-B sleeping quarters was a lagoon, with a
dozen cots anchored along each bank. Everything was
still, even the little H's, this due to the nature of the bed-
ding. The army cots they slept upon were preposterously narrow; the slightest movement invited a shipwreck
for the occupant. Two steel-framed panels flanked each
cot, the canvass on them tauter than sails in a hurricane.
When not in use, the panels hung limply off the sides,
like Bormann's arms after Hitler told him to stop trawl-
ing his pockets for oysters. For sleeping purposes, however, the panels were hiked up and locked into a hori-
zontal position, where they jutted out level with the
main body of the cot. They could support *some* weight
– a toe, maybe a stray elbow, but little more. Anyone
careless enough to favor either port or starboard, or lash
out at a nightmare leviathan, or, worse, attempt to roll
over, would in an instant cause the whole gizmo to cap-
size like a torpedoed dinghy.

I was about to take my leave, when I heard the faintest
squeaks. Who would dare be fidgeting? I peered over at the
source of the noise, the third cot on the left. It was vibrating ever
so slightly. On closer inspection, I identified Goldi sleeping there.

Well, not sleeping, exactly.

Lying on her stomach, under a gray blanket, the pudgy secretary was jilling off. Her face was scrunched up as if in agony, her eyes slit in steely resolve. Her pillow was nowhere to be found; ditto her hands. To judge by the hurly burly going on at her midsection – the motions called to mind a village woman, scrubbing her husband's longjohns on a rock by the creek – I knew the missing pillow was getting a grade A work-out.

I took in the free show. I had seen human self-love enacted before, but I had not realized the female of the species engaged in this behavior. My gaze drifted to the space below the cot, the middle of which, every half-second, nearly touched the floor. There, something caught my eye: a small book. Perhaps it is true what they say about cats and curiosity, for I risked being crushed like a walnut for a glimpse of what was in that book.

"The Dark Exception"

You're the prettiest
Girl I've ever seen
Who wasn't drawn, or
In a magazine

Not Goethe, but not bad. The poem was inscribed on an unlined sheet of paper. I found it tucked inside the front cover of the book, which turned out to be Goldi's diary.[25]

---

[25] Before anyone gets up on their hind legs to object that I violated the lady's privacy, I say in my own defense that I was only looking for clues as to how I might better ingratiate myself with der Führer. Besides, she never once fed me.

At the bottom right of the page was written the initial, "A."

The diary itself was penned as if by a love-starved schoolgirl (loopy handwriting, generous doses of exclamation marks, tiny hearts dotting the i's). A typical passage: "Does he really care for me? Would a relationship with him have a future, or am I setting myself up for Weep City, like with that 'deserting' fox, Rommel? Does the poem mean what I think it means? Maybe he just wants me to dye my hair blonde!!! And what does he plan to do about Princess Eva? Ach, I'm such a fool for being in love with him!!!"

Forty pages of such tripe cured my insomnia, but good. The two-legs and their "romance" – yawn. When I left, to curl up in the janitor's closet atop some soft rags, Goldi was still scrubbing the longjohns.

. . .

Over the next several weeks, and despite the official ban on a free press, word of military setbacks seeped into the bunker. Newspaper headlines, had they reflected reality, would have arrived each dawn like a screaming judo kick in the gut.

Landsberg, Bartenstein Fall to Russkis
Bartensberg, Landstein Next?

22 U-Boats Sunk by Yanks
We Nailed Maybe Two of Theirs, Tops

Siegfried Line Broken
Why Won't Ref Stop This Fight?

Nazis Bounced from Belgium like Beatnik Barflies
Brussels Mayor: "And Stay Out!"

Brits Fly 800 Lancaster Bombers to Dresden
RAF "War Pigeons" Crap Fire All Night Long

Even Canadians Whomping Us Now
Reach Rhine, Eh

Roosevelt, Churchill, Stalin: "Victory is Assured"
Leaders at Yalta Mostly Talk Dames, Roadsters

By early March, the air inside our little hole in the ground, never spring meadow fresh to begin with, had grown dense and clammy; the expressions of those around me suggested the bunker had taken on an excess of gravity. Although it would have been heresy to openly suggest we might lose the war, we all knew that for the foreseeable future sunglasses would not be needed, except possibly as kindling. The Goebbels brats, for instance, had been enduring taunts from schoolmates, the gist of which was that the Red Army would hang them by the thumbs inside of three months. When one of the smaller H's asked his mother what "hanging" was, the blotto Magda drew him a picture (literally). Much bawling and lederhosen-wetting ensued.

More troubling still, the bad news was a manure in which bickering between my master and mistress mushroomed.

One morning in the bedroom, Hitler was grooming himself in front of the mirror. He combed the right side, he combed the left side. He combed and combed, and the more he combed, the more irate he grew. He turned away from the mirror and lit up a Lucky Strike. Then he looked at Fräulein Braun, who was petting me on the bed while reading an old copy of Julius Streicher's rag, *Der Stürmer*. After a minute of exhaling sullen puffs of smoke, he blurted, "I am, aren't I?"

"I told you," she sighed, turning a page. "I don't know. And please use the ashtray. I can never find that maid to clean up anymore."

"Verdammt! You didn't even look!"

"Don't swear at me! And I'm sure it hasn't changed in the last five minutes."

"So, I *am* going bald?"

"'Going bald' is for head hair. *Not* upper-lip hair."

"What, now you're writing a grammar column for the newspaper?"

"I think cigarettes make you hyper. Why don't you get some smack? You're always nicer after some good smack. Ask Hermann to get you some smack."

"Never mind that fat manatee! We're talking about me! Look at the picture on the dresser!" he continued. "That was just *one year* ago!"

"So maybe you *are* going bald! It's a moustache! Shave it off! I never liked it anyway. And if *I* don't like it," she said, "then *who* exactly are you keeping it for?"

"You never liked – since when? You used to say when we were first going out –"

"I said a lot of things. 'Gosh, Dolfi, your moustache is a dream! Ooh, Dolfi, these new uniforms *really* turn me on! And oh yes, we have to murder all the Hebes, ASAP!'"

Hitler took in his girlfriend as if for the first time. "What's gotten into you?"

"This ridiculous article, for one thing. Did you know that Jews are the cause of floods? That the Jewish race began when devils fornicated with monkeys? That people never sneezed until Jews came along? That kosher meat is really German babies? That –"

"Get to the point, woman!"

"Well. You've probably explained it before. So forgive me for making you repeat yourself. But just *why* is it that we're all supposed to hate Jews so fricken much?"

Der Führer pointed to the book case, the five shelves of which contained some two hundred remaindered copies of the same leather-bound volume. "Read my book!"

She sighed. "*Mein Kamel?* Frankly, the subject matter doesn't interest me. Maybe if I ever visit the Sahara, and need to rent some transportation –"

"It's *Kampf*, not *Kamel!* And it was a best-seller, I'll have you know!"

I did not catch what Fräulein Braun said next, partly because she said it under her breath, and partly because she was just then stroking my ears; Hitler, apparently, heard it.

"No one was 'forced' to buy it! Where in hell do you get off … Ach, I'm going to find someone else to talk to!"

"Ja," said Fräulein Braun, after he had left, "And I'll bet I know who. Even you know who, don't you, Tutti?"

Sure do, I said to myself, as she kissed the back of my head.

The tension was upsetting, but it did lead my lonely mistress to show me more kindness. I was never fed so well as when she and Hitler argued.

When Frau Schultz was sent for, with a bowl of chopped up, no-spit ham, I knew the decision at Auschwitz had been the right one.

Schadenfreude

One advantage I held over the bitch was that I was the pet privileged to sit in on Hitler's psychotherapy sessions. (The level of discussion was naturally way over her pudding head, and after a minute Blondi would stare at the door, whining to be let out.). The conversations between Hitler and Dr. Schadenfreude afforded me invaluable insight into der Führer's most intimate hang-ups, one of with which I already had a passing acquaintance: his inability to perform in the sack.[26]

The historians typically call Hitler a genius of communications. While this bromide held with respect to large crowds, in one-on-one jobs the crossed wires he encountered often left people flabbergasted. Once, he broached the subject of his sexual difficulties with his shrink. He began in an agonizingly roundabout way, describing his first playground kiss, then segueing into dreams of trains and tunnels, giant zippers with sharp metal teeth, and finally Albert Einstein in a two-piece women's bathing suit, winking impishly while juggling kielbasas and chanting, "They're good with mustard!"

When Hitler got to the point ("I can't schtup!"), Dr. Schadenfreude tried to divine if the problem's roots were physio- or psychological. He asked his patient about his eating and drinking habits, and then if he indulged in tobacco.

---

[26] I would, on the evenings Hitler futilely ordered his private to stand at attention, slink out of the bedroom and leave it to Fräulein Braun to confront the terrible aftermath alone.

"Tobacco!" Hitler winced testily, as if a child had just asked him if pigs could tap dance. "Relevance, please?"

The doctor's response, lamentably, was misheard by der Führer, who gleaned that smoking in some cases was known to cause *omni*potence. Thereafter, hazy blue smoke and hacking coughs permeated the bunker bedroom.

In another session, the communication question was front and center. Hitler was in denial about his shortcomings in this area, and persisted in ascribing blame to others. About the Italian high command, he said, "You think *I* can't get my point across? What about those mortadella munchers, Doc? Always with the hands! You offer them a drink, they smile and point to their lips. You ask them the time, they hold up three fingers and a bent thumb – three-thirty, I *guess!* And try extracting information about something more complex, like how the offensives are going in Greece or North Africa. Forget it! You'd have to give them ten kilos of soft clay and let them sculpt for a week!"

The assassination attempts had begun to irk him as well, and made him feel as if no one were on his side. "No one?" Doctor Schadenfreude said. "What about Fräulein Braun?"

"Eva's a big nag. And okay, she's *always* nagged me, but it's not cute anymore. Do you know what she's accusing me of now? She – ach, I don't want to talk about it. Next!"

"What about your lieutenants? Albert Speer seems like a thoughtful young man."

"Slowly? We used to rap all night. Architecture, philosophy, ponies. Now it's just, 'The Theresienstadt. Factory has. Fallen fifty-two. Percent behind. On bullet.

Production, mein. Führer.' Gloom and doom, that's all I get from Slowly these days. Did he ever think to ask, 'How are you. Feeling, mein. Führer? Would you like. To join the wife and. Me. For dinner and. Charades this. Saturday?' Just a little human touch, know what I mean?"

"Yes, of course," Doctor Schadenfreude nodded, taking notes. "Everyone needs companionship. If in times of need you can't unburden yourself to a friend, you become a cannibal of your own heart."

"No poetry!"

"Sorry, mein Führer. What about the others? The Reich Marshall? You two have been friends for, what, over twenty years?"

"Göring!" Hitler thundered. "Used to be a barrel of laughs, now he's just a barrel of lard! Goebbels and H2 are fine as far as a working relationship goes, but they're dead inside. Bormann and 'von' Ribbentrop would stab each other in the eyeballs for the chance to smell my armpits, and lately I wonder if that's even a good thing. And that's just what I have at home! What about abroad!" Hitler sat up on the couch and grew more animated. "Where are the loyal puppet leaders of yesteryear? Oh, the Yanks just *had* to liberate France! Those Frenchies were the best collaborators we ever had! Better even than the Slovaks and Croats, who, one mustn't forget, are stinking Slavs. How brutal those gendarmes could be!"

"Yes, but I was thinking more along the lines of –"

"Cripes, over in Italy, a so-*called* fascist state, those soft-hearted Dagos were trying to *protect* the prisoners! Some pals *they* are! And their delicate sense of aesthetics was always offended! Too much garlic in the pasta sauce! Not enough give in the German jackboot! Verdammt, you couldn't even sit back and watch any good torture footage with them – they'd always ream out the director for the lousy 'montaggio!'"

"Mein Führer," Doctor Schadenfreude said, suppressing a chuckle, "it sounds to me like, where the Italians are concerned, you have an *axis* to grind!"

"Hey, no puns! I *hate* puns! *No* poetry, and *no* puns! Got it? Verdammt, you're supposed to be a *professional* over here!"

"Just a little levity, you know. I thought it would help to, ah … Please continue."

"'Axis to grind.' Sheesh!"

"Ja, I apologize. Go on."

"Okay, I will." Hitler eyed the doctor coldly for a second, and then lay down again, back in patient mode. "Now, the Swiss, I have no use for those neutral yodellers. I could have invaded them at any time, but what's the point? It'd be like beating up a shower curtain! *France!* Now *that* was a pleasure to invade! Alsace-Lorraine, eh? I'll give them Alsace-Lorainne … *right up the wagon!* Sign right here on the dotted line, Monsieur! Pah! Oh ja, those frogs were remarkably accommodating. The one place I never had to send little Dolfi Eichmann, no sir. That's why I didn't blow Paris back to the Stone Age! Because over there, when it came to the Big J question, the Frenchies were on the same page as us!"

"I'm glad you brought that up," the doctor said, taking a sip of schnapps. "As I think you'd agree, we've made progress with the argyles."

"Ja," Hitler said, cagily. "Is this about money? I told you, the payroll guy's a tyrant. He won't authorize any new expenses unless – "

"No, mein Führer, it's not that. I was merely going to suggest that, since we've moved beyond the socks, perhaps we can tackle your unhealthy obsession with the Jews."

Hitler pulled the plug on that, pronto. "You too, Doc? I'm sick of explaining it to everyone. Read my book!"[27]

• • •

My reconnaissance tours continued, but circumstances prevented me from knowing everything. There were shut doors. There were events that unfolded outside the bunker. There was also the twenty hours a day of sleep that I required. Therefore, it was difficult to determine precisely how far the Hitler and Goldi affair had gone. Clearly, something was in the air. Fräulein Braun, too, had become more suspicious.

"Was it the secretary?" she once asked, waking both der Führer and me. She had turned on her night-light to grill him about who had hooked him on cigarettes. "I'll bet it was the secretary. The fat one who smokes like a café existentialist."

"She's not fat. She's plump," was Hitler's sleepy-eyed, ill-advised, retort.

"Plump?" Now Fräulein Braun leaned over and turned on the night-light on *his* side of the bed. Hitler yanked the blanket up over his head, knocking me to the floor. "Plump, huh? Five-three, a hundred and fifty pounds, that's *fat*, any way you look at it! Except maybe

27 Had he survived the war, Doctor Schadenfreude could have provided keen observations into the workings of Hitler's mind. Sadly, a few days before the final carnage in the bunker Blondi confused the doctor with Stalin. For the last time, Mengele paid a visit with his black leather bag.

through a lover's eyes!"

"Herr Gott! Get that fricken spotlight outta my fricken face!"

"Was it sexy, her showing you how to hold a cigarette?"

"Are you nuts? What are –"

"And when you coughed like a Welsh coal miner after the first puff, did she giggle coquettishly and pat your back?"

"Giggle? First puff! *What* Welsh coal miner? I have no idea what –"

"Don't deny it! Who do you think you're talking to, Neville fricken Chamberlain?"

The accusations exploded and ricocheted off the walls like a tossed carton of Egg 39 hand grenades.

I ducked out of the line of fire. At the door, I indicated, subtly, that I wanted out. I was freed fifteen long minutes later, when Hitler flung open the door to escape himself.

As we walked, ticked off and tired, down the corridor together, he on his way to the washroom for a Lucky Strike and I to the janitor's closet for some peace, I cursed his vanity. The entire brouhaha could have been avoided if he had told the truth about the smoking, that he was doing it to make his schwanz more cucumber-like and less wet noodle-like, and that it was not the secretary but Doctor Schadenfreude who had (inadvertently) started him on the path to black lungs. Was Blondi's stupidity contagious?

• • •

The threat of violence was yet another impediment

to the gathering of information. There were some in the bunker who, given the flimsiest of pretenses, would gleefully put their boots to me.

"Stop staring at me! Stop trying to hypnotize me!"

BOOT!

"*You* again! What did I tell you about spreading your cooties in my kitchen! *Raus*, you dirty beast! Or I'll boil you in this pot and tell everyone it's wild hare!"

BOOT!

"Hey! You're telepathically communicating to Goebbels which cards I'm holding in my hand, aren't you?"

BOOT!

What is more, the person who booted me most did not even do so intentionally. She was but an extreme example of the congenital oafishness of *Homo sapiens*.

When compared to the feline, the average human is graceless. Except in degrees, his method of motion does not progress beyond that of a toddler stumbling through his first few steps. (A cat could look so ungainly only when rendered senseless by catnip or a head injury.) Here he goes, putting his left foot out and hoping for the best. The extended leg stiffens. For a moment all is balanced on the right foot, which calls out, "Hello? Why am I holding this building up all by my lonesome? I'm not even centered!" The left heel, as in the figures found on school crossing signs, lightly touches down. Inertial mass carries the rest of the body forward, until the left sole thwacks the ground. "A safe landing!" the left foot cries in relief. "Scheiße, that was close!" "But wait a minute!" the right foot exclaims. "Now *I'm* airborne! Hello? Hello?"

In case you think I am singling out two-legs for criticism, let me say that there are those in the four-leg community who will never be mistaken for prize-winning ballroom dancers, either. Dogs come to mind. From the instant, as witless little puppies, that they can stand of their own free will, they clomp around and bound about. Surely you have observed them in parks and woodlands, clomping, bounding, bounding, clomping – pausing briefly to bite a flea off their tails – then bounding and clomping again, always driven more by a crude and giddy "love of life" than physical artistry.

When their paws hit the ground, they do so with force. They *try* to be noisy, the equivalent of the human throat-clearing which announces, "I'm here! Notice me! Please don't leave me alone with my thoughts, for I haven't any!"

When galumphing on grass, dirt, or gravel, they cannot help but squeeze some of the surface into their paws. And they leave tracks – everywhere you find the graffiti of their pads, toes, and claws (the last of which have not even evolved to the point of being retractable). A dog is pushy and vulgar, an old blowhard in a long check-out line who stands too close and assumes you want to be friends as much as he does, and regardless of your species will jam his snout into your crotch for a good, deep sniff.

Now observe the cat. He places his paw down daintily. Each footfall is a tiny wonder, so sleek and epicurean, a classy geisha girl at the top of her game. Aside from surfaces covered in snow or dust, you will never see where he has been. He moves slowly, elegantly, with a corporeal majesty, a warm spring breeze that caresses your cheeks, and scents them with lilacs. And do not be taken in by outward appearances, for this seemingly lackadaisical creature can, when conditions warrant, go from 0 to 60 in the blink of an eye.

Which brings us back to the Kaiserine of Klutz.

It was an afternoon in March. (As it represented the apex of my bunker stay, I recall the date perfectly: 18 March, 1945). The two secretaries were stinking up the lunchroom with Lucky Strikes on yet another one of their extended breaks. Alice sat alone at the dining table, frowning, while her colleague worked. Goldi had rolled in a wheeled desk, on top of which was a sewing machine; scattered around it were spools of thread, patterns clipped from ladies' magazines, a green velvet material, and a tin ashtray.

"A date with der Führer, huh?" Alice said, not sounding at all impressed.

Goldi sat hunched over the machine, puffing excitedly while her foot clacked the treadle on the floor. "He's taking me to a jazz club! Erich's driving us, after midnight. Our first date, Missi! A *jazz* club! Downtown! I feel like a *movie* star! He says it's full of decadent Negro music that poisons the mind and corrupts the soul, but that the highballs are terrific. I hope this dress turns out okay. Every dress I have makes my popo look big!"

"What about Eva?"

Goldi was too preoccupied with the hem to catch the censure in Alice's tone. "He's going to leave her soon, once things settle down a bit. You know, with the B-17's shelling us all day. Or is it the B-29's? He says it would disrupt the war effort if they broke up now."

"If you ask me, it sounds just like the line Rommel was feeding you."

Goldi lifted her foot off the treadle, and into the sudden silence asked, "You think?" But she was not interested in Alice's opinion, for she absentmindedly plucked out the thread from where it had got stuck in the material, and resumed clacking.

"Well, I guess it's up to you," Alice said, her shaking head quietly tacking on the word *dummy.*

Goldi got up and walked to the ice box. On the way there, she *booted* me! Even though I was sitting under a chair! And she did not even notice!

I moved out of her path, but on the return trip the heel of her black pumps somehow spiked me. I let out a yowl; this startled her and caused *her* to let out a much louder yowl!

"Cripes, that beast scared me! I didn't even know it was here! What's it *doing* in here? It's always underfoot when we're girl-talking! What, is it spying for Eva? I wouldn't put it past her! And why am I always stepping on it?"

Because you're a clumsy lummox, I wanted to shout.

As I went to door, on my way to see how Hitler was handling the upcoming date, Goldi *did it again!* Somehow she had taken a few quick steps behind me and stumbled, and *again* booted me, and *again* spiked my tail, in the *exact same spot!*

After convalescing with a short nap, I headed to Hitler's bedroom. I found him sitting up in bed, smoking and re-reading a passage from *Mein Kampf.* (Fräulein Braun was gone for the night, to visit a sick aunt in Potsdam.) Several times he whispered to himself, "It's so clear! How could anyone *not* get it?"

I gingerly hopped up on the bed, trying to gauge der Führer's mood with respect to lying at his feet. He quickly parted his legs to make room.

After a few minutes he yawned and checked his

watch, perhaps calculating how much time he had until the rendevous with Goldi. He dropped his cigarette in the ashtray, got up, returned the book to the shelf, and closed the door. Then he climbed back into bed, turned off the night-light, and settled in for a little lie-down.

We slept for perhaps half an hour. The bunker was rocked by some distant shelling, and objects rattled in cabinets and on dresser tops. As this happened every day (courtesy of the American carpet-bombers) and night (the RAF incendiary bombers), we paid it no mind.

I awoke to a sweltering orange inferno. A bomb had dislodged Hitler's cigarette from the ashtray (he had not yet cottoned on to stubbing the butts out completely), and it had fallen, still lit, onto a leather rug. Some useless instinct impelled me to leap onto my sleeping master's face. I was so panicked that my claws were extended, and I scratched him across the fore-head, leaving several deep cuts. Before even opening his eyes he unleashed a backhander that launched me like a dinner plate against the wall. I thought I heard a couple of ribs crack, but I counted myself lucky that he had aimed me at the portion of the room that was not engulfed in flames.

"Fricken hell! Now the damn *cat's* trying to assassi-nate me!"

In short order he grasped the situation. Springing out of bed, he pulled off the leather blanket and tossed it over the fire, smothering the threat. Then he put on his slippers and stomped out the fading embers.

Panting, he turned to me. I was limping back and forth by the door, trying to walk off my charley horse. "Mein Gott! You saved my life, Muffi!"

He still did not know my name – but for all I cared

he could stick a feather up my nosehole and call me Macaroni! No, what mattered was the way he was gazing down on me, with heartfelt gratitude etched all over his blood-soaked face.

I had done it! I had won his love! *Rapture!*

Yes, I had pounced on his face out of pure fear, but *he* thought it was to deliver him from the hot hand of Death. And who knows, maybe somewhere in the back of my mind that was the real ... no, it was pure fear.

But so what! I *deserved* this! And somehow it was all the sweeter for having come after weeks and weeks of fruitless scheming.[28] Hurrah, serendipity!

The next few hours were the most remarkable of my life. Der Führer, after hastily wrapping a tourniquet around his forehead, stroked me tenderly, tickled my chin, and rubbed his moustache against my nose (it *did* feel like it was going bald). Best of all, he whispered into my ear that *I* was his favorite pet!

Then he scooped me up and carried me to the kitchen.[29]

There, he plied me with the crème de la crème, kicking off the feast with an apéritif of crème; then, an appetizer of le poulet rôtisserie; and finally the main course, les chops de pork. So filled was der Führer with

[28] I have gone into detail only for Operation Samstag, but there were several other efforts that did not pan out. Most notable among them were Operation Freitag (same principle), Operation Dog Poo Under the Pillow, and Operation Imitation Barking in the Wee Hours.

[29] Hitler's inexperience at holding a cat showed, as he squeezed me much too tightly; his eager grip was a vise that severely constricted my breathing. But I did not protest. Nor did I complain when, without due notice, he dropped me to the floor from rather too great a height.

joie de vivre (I will stop now with the faux French) that
he even went so far as to wave Frau Schultz off when
she started pulling pots off their hooks. He ripped off
her leather apron and fastened it on, insisting on
preparing my food himself.[30]

In addition to the cook, milling about us were a
few guards, the secretaries, Kempka, Fräulein Müller,
and, of course, Bormann. While I stuffed my face like
an Egyptian cat goddess, they were regaled with the
story of our leader's rescue. Except for Bormann, who
was jealous, and Frau Schultz, who was just plain
mean, everyone seemed to be very proud of me. They
patted my back and said things like, "Nice job, Muffi!"
(Most knew my real name, but did not want to con-
tradict der Führer.)

The highlight, fittingly, involved my rival. Blondi
had caught a whiff of my meal and galloped into the
kitchen. Upon entry, which involved a sharp left turn,
she lost traction and slid across the floor, making for a
dull *clonk* as her skull collided with the wood stove.
The welt on her head, predictably, did little to dampen
her dumb dog enthusiasm. When she spotted my eats
she trotted over and, with her big snout, nudged me
roughly off the bowl.

How did I react? I played the gentleman caller who
has just been vomited on by his new ladyfriend's baby
niece – I stepped aside, and good-naturedly licked some
pork grease from my lips. Why be miffed? Unlike Blondi,
I had recently looked up at the scoreboard, and for the
first time Team Tutti was out in front.

Before one drop of the bitch's saliva contaminated

[30] He was a damn fine cook, too – he did not bludgeon the meat's
natural goodness with all kinds of superfluous spices.

the bowl, der Führer collared her roughly. I thought he was going to break her neck!

"Huh?" she barked. "Huh? Huh?"

"Scheiße! *Now* you're barking?" der Führer erupted. "You were right outside the door when the bedroom was baking like Dresden! Why didn't you bark then?"

And then he swatted her. Right on the snout. And when she stared back at him with her hopelessly dim eyes, he swatted her again! The message at last reached her pea brain, and she slunk out of the kitchen. It was all I could do to keep from somersaulting!

Whoever directs the moving picture of my life will surely, for the scene I have just recounted, instruct his cameraman to smear the lens with a drop of vaseline, thus creating a soft, hazy focus that, however clichéd, effectively transports the viewer to a dream world. And it really *was* a wonderful dream!

Until the cowfish washed ashore.

Göring was hopped up on smack. Hitler, who did not notice or care, again related the events of the blaze. The Reich Marshall smiled and nodded his head as if he were enjoying the tale immensely. Hitler concluded with, "So what do you say, Tubby? How about taking off one of those medals and pinning it on Muffi here."

"Well, mein Führer," the Reich Marshall began, "before I unfasten any medals, I have a question. During the fire, was the bedroom door open, or closed?"

Hitler looked confused. "Closed, of course. I was asleep."

Göring grinned. "I see. The door was closed. The room was on fire. This cat," he said, pointing at me (I had stopped eating, my appetite suddenly gone), "was therefore trapped in a burning room. The only way out for him was to wake you and have *you* open the door for *him*. Therefore, if it pleases der Führer, I would be happy to give *you* one of my medals for saving the life of this cat."

Göring was still grinning, and Bormann was trying to hide a smile, but the rest of the room was looking at the floor, Hitler included. The explanation was not true, but it was easy to see that der Führer believed it, and now felt silly for the way he had acted. Embarrassment gave way to anger, and he bent down to where I still sat and shoved me away from the pork chops. Then he snatched the bowl, and empted it into a garbage can.

"All right, you've had your fun," he said to Göring.

The smack must have been wreaking havoc with the Reich Marshall's judgement, for he refused to drop the matter. "Mein Führer, you really are a dope."

The fat pufferfish was crossing a line, and everyone knew it.

Göring lifted his hand, and, with his fingers pinching Hitler's noseholes, said, "Verdammt! Your noseholes! They're *gone!* Some villain has stolen your noseholes! How will you breathe without your noseholes?" He pulled his hand away, and with his open palm presented the noseholes for all to see. "Why, there they are! I found your noseholes! Now, where is my medal?" He laughed at his own joke, as only one addled on drugs could.

The room had fallen silent. Hitler took a step forward, his "saved" noseholes flaring. In an instant all color drained from his face (a nifty trick, that). He hissed, "How about you and me step outside, and settle this monkey to monkey?"

Göring recovered his wits enough to grovel. He stuttered an apology, and then patted der Führer's chest in an obeisant manner that suggested, "Hey, come on, *you're* the dominant monkey around here, big guy. I was just having a little fun, that's all."

"All right, then," Hitler said, the matter settled. To Kempka, he added, "Is the limo ready to go?"

"Go where, mein Führer?" Bormann squealed in alarm.

"Doesn't concern you, Marti. Goldi and I are ... going to a meeting. It's not important. You wouldn't be interested."

"I – I wouldn't be *interested?* But mein Führer, I exist only to serve –"

"Only to serve me, I know, I know." Hitler cast a guilty glance around the room, before his gaze fell on Goldi in her new green dress (specifically, the rub-a-dub-dub of her big chunky hams – what a popo!). "We'll talk tomorrow, Marti."

Once everyone else had cleared out, I tipped over the garbage can. In the dark, I finished my cold meal.

• • •

Early the following morning, I heard all about the date.

I had set up camp in the Bergen-Belsen sleeping quarters, under a newly-unoccupied cot next to Alice's (several days before, yet another guard had been hauled before a firing squad because Blondi mistook him for Stalin). I figured that after the rescue fiasco Hitler would not be too keen on parting his feet for me in bed. I also figured that Goldi would dish the dirt on her date two seconds after her arrival. On the latter count, I was proven correct.

Goldi rushed in and crouched at her colleague's cot,

whispering excitedly. "Missi, it was aces!" The cool night air and time with Hitler had had a salubrious effect on the secretary: black eyes gleaming, cheeks reddened and alive. "First, we got out in an alley about a block from the club. He didn't want the limo to draw attention to us. You know, snipers and such. Then, to be incognito, he borrowed dark glasses and a fedora from Erich. Also an ascot, but for some reason it was *really* dirty, so Dolfi didn't want to wear it."

"Oh," Alice said, grumpily rubbing her tired eyes, "it's 'Dolfi' now, is it?"

"Well, ja. I know he's still my boss and everything, but I'm not going to call my boyfriend 'der Führer' – at least not behind his back. Just to his face."

"Ja. So, anyway."

"Ja. So, anyway, we're standing in line, listening to the bebop blaring inside. It got pretty cold, out there on the sidewalk. It's one of those clubs where you have to wait until you catch the doorman's eye? And then he decides if you're hep enough to get in."

"Hep?"

"It's slang. So after about fifteen minutes Dolfi got impatient and just grabbed my shoulder and pushed us through the crowd. People were, like, 'Hey, big shot! Who do you think you are, der Führer?' Which is pretty funny when you think about it, since he *is* –"

"I can figure out why it's funny, thanks."

"Are you mad at me or something?"

Neither of them spoke for a minute, until Alice said, "Never mind. Go on."

"Well, we got to the door, and this bouncer stopped us. He just held up his hands and said, 'Nein!' So, real fast-like, Dolfi leaned in, tipped up his hat and glasses, and said, 'Psst! Günther! It's me.'"

"Günther? As in Frau Schultz's son?"

"Different Günther. Anyway, we got in, and the host seated us at a table right by the bandstand. Oh, Missi! We drank highballs, and laughed, and made fun of other people's clothes! What a *swell* night! I felt like Carole Lombarde! Every now and then someone would approach him for an autograph. Well, you know how he is around *here* when he's interrupted, but *there* he was all smiles! Really, he's a such down-to-earth guy! Did you know he was just a regular foot soldier back in the Great War?"

"Everyone knows that, Goldi."

"Anyway, it was nice. Just … getting to know each other." She sighed, contented.

"Did he do the argyle spiel? And the one about the Jews?"

"Ja, but I sat those out in the powder room."

There was a short pause, and then Alice said, "You made out with him, didn't you?"

"A little bit," Goldi giggled.

"Second base?"

"Third."

A truncated gasp escaped Alice's lips. "Scheiße, Goldi! Oral?"

"Don't look so shocked! It just … *happened*. We had a good buzz on, especially after we switched over to the schnapps. And then when we got back to the alley, well, Erich was dozing at the wheel, so we stopped and looked up at the moon for a while. You know, between the bombed-out buildings. Oh, Missi, it was *so* romantic!"

"And?"

"I thought we were just going to neck a little. But when I went to kiss him, he got all weird, and yelled, 'Don't mess up my moustache!'"

"What's *that* mean?"

"No idea. But then he unbuttoned his trousers, and pushed my head down there."

"Oh, mein Gott!"

"And if I may say so, I equipped myself *very* well. And he was a real gentleman after. He didn't insult me or slap me around. You know, like Rommel used to. He just patted my head and handed me his handkerchief to spit into."

"Oh, mein Gott!"

"Do you want to know how big he is?"

"Don't be gross!"

"Suit yourself."

"How big is he?"

"*Big* – wicked big. My jaw still hurts. Except ... well ... I really shouldn't –"

"What? What!"

"Well, this is kind of ... unusual. But he only had one ... you know."

"Only one?"

"Ja. I asked him if that meant we couldn't ever have any little Dolfis."

"And?"

"And he lost his stiffy, for about a minute. Made me promise never to bring the subject up again."

• • •

That same afternoon, Hitler put into effect his scorched earth policy.

In the lunchroom, where the announcement was

made, his lieutenants stared in quiet disbelief – except for Göring, whose noisy annihilation of the chili continued unabated.

"What, no standing ovation?" Hitler asked. "You guys depress me. No spirit. No get-up-and-go. *Göring, drop that spoon!* You know what? We should change the name of the Nazi Party to 'the Dead End Kids,' because that's what you losers are – dead ends! Hiya, Dead End Kids! Hiya, Bim! Hiya, Hunky! Hiya, Patsy! Hiya, Crab! Cripes, I oughta shoot you all in the neck!"

"But, mein Führer," Goebbels said at last, "it just seems so – I don't know – I mean, a *scorched earth* policy? Can we even *do* that?"

"'Can we even *do* that?'" Hitler bellowed. "We're the fricken government! It'll be as easy as taking babies from a whore named Candy!"

Exodus

Day and night, enemy planes streaked the Berlin sky with plunging target markers, leaving fuzzy ropes of smoke hanging from the clouds. As the Russkis pasted us from the east, and the Yanks and Brits from the west, Hitler discovered who his true friends were.

Göring was the first to break ranks. He deserted one night (*after* dinner, of course), saying he was going out to buy gum. First, he decorated himself in all his ribbons and medals, so that he looked like the Vatican Christmas tree. Then, after Kempka helped to pack him in behind the wheel of a jeep, he drove through the garden gates for the last time.

The fat sea cow's intention had been to surrender to the Yanks, and then charm them into granting him political asylum, or at least some chicken wings. He stopped at the first US army unit he found. In the midst of giving himself up, he lugged three six-packs of beer and some of Frau Schultz's homemade pretzels from the back seat, all the while singing the song he had been rehearsing for the occasion (for at least three days before he left, he filled the bunker halls with his booming baritone: *"He's the boogie woogie bugle boy of Company B."*) The Yanks were not buying, and slapped handcuffs on him – although they drank the beer, ate the pretzels, and perhaps even enjoyed the numbers (Göring was no Kempka, but he could carry a tune).[31]

When the Russkis began to shell Potsdamer Platz, just two blocks from the bunker, Himmler lost his nerve and began to shake like a cheap kite in a tornado. Two nights after Göring jumped ship, the Reich Leader of the SS fled the bunker, on the same pretext: to buy gum. He had prior to this managed to finagle a German passport from a local female impersonator; that is to say, he planned to slip past Allied checkpoints by impersonating a female impersonator. The scheme collapsed when Himmler, in his acute panic, got so spun around that he ended up impersonating a *male* impersonator impersonating *Himmler*. A British guard easily saw through the disguise, which was in fact no disguise at all. The ex-chicken farmer took his own life two days later during a routine medical exam, using a tiny crumb of Frau Göring's strudel that he had been concealing beneath a false tooth.

The defections knocked der Führer for a loop, and his paranoia deepened.

One day, not long after Doctor Schadenfreude had been put down, Hitler was alone in the library, lying on his black leather therapy couch. When I strolled in to have a peek at the paper, I barely recognized him. He was hitting the schnapps real hard. His swastika armband had a big ketchup stain on it. He was disheveled, unshaven, and clicking his teeth uncontrollably; he looked like an sleep-deprived Fagin.

---

[31] Much of this account is gleaned from testimony that emerged at the Nuremberg trial, where the Reich Marshall, with ten of his co-defendants, was sentenced to death. Awaiting execution in his cell, Göring, ever the sly one, cheated the hangman when he swallowed a piece of his wife's strudel that had been smuggled in to him.

"Ach, Muffi," der Führer cried. He was as drunk and weepy as an Irishman on the anniversary of his mother's death. "Ach, mein little cat."

Was he finally ready to reach out and love me?

Fat chance. "Go find Blondi," he sobbed. "Mein Gott, I need Blondi!"

Find her yourself, I thought, and then went back to reading the theater reviews.

Aside from Goldi, whose designs on Hitler blinded her to the harsh reality around her, and the dog, who was thrilled just so long as she could slather her spit over something, no one was holding up well. Kempka had discarded his snazzy threads in favor of the Michigan State sweatshirt he now wore at all times. Fräulein Braun canceled her subscriptions to *Vogue* and *Kierkegaard Today*, and stopped shaving her legs and moustache (the latter soon grew nearly as thick as Hitler's own, a consequence that plagued him and clearly amused her). After learning of Himmler's demise, the remaining bigwigs – Goebbels, Bormann, "von" Ribbentrop, and Speer – put on brave faces, and vowed never to resort to the "Strudel Solution" (as everyone holed up in the bunker was now calling it).

• • •

21 April, 1945.

Der Führer's birthday. I knew, by mid-morning, that there would be mayhem that evening. Half an hour apart, I had overhead a scatter-brained Hitler promise both Goldi and Fräulein Braun that he would spend the night celebrating with each.

Hitler's carelessness at keeping his affairs in order

was due in part to his worries. Early that morning, he received word that several of Zhukov's leading tank units had reached the eastern suburbs of Berlin. Goebbels and Speer had brought the radio to Hitler in the cafeteria. The four of us listened intently as the broadcaster, between snippets of Wagner, repeated the news every fifteen minutes.

After the third such update – "They're here, folks! Break out the Russki dictionaries and start grovelling!" – Hitler grabbed hold of the radio and threw it to the floor, smashing it to pieces. "Some birthday this is turning out to be!"

Goebbels looked at Speer. Speer shrugged. The Propaganda Minister, as he had done a million times before, dove into the task of raising der Führer's spirits. "Valor always, defeat never! Brave Nazi soldiers to fight back Slavic onslaught! Ivan will be crushed! Deutschland to Stalin: your popo is ours! The battle is –"

"Shaddup!" Hitler shouted. "You know you make me dizzy when you talk in headlines! Cripes, I can't breathe in here! Everybody beat it! Slowly, bring me Blondi, and Goebbels, take this damn cat outta here!"

I can show myself out, I thought, and trotted by Goebbels's outstretched arms.

I walked down the corridor, and through the passage that divided the bunker. It had been a long time since anyone had given me a tasty treat, and I was hoping Kempka or the maid would be about. Before I found either, I came to a stop outside the B-B washroom. Familiar voices emanated from within. I pressed my ear to the door.

Goldi: "I told him to dump Eva this afternoon. Make

a clean break on his birthday. He's fifty-six, right? Time to grow up. Kick her out of here, or maybe just give her my old job. At any rate, that cot's doing a mean number on my lumbago. I think I've put in enough time as a secretary."

Alice: "What's that supposed to mean?"

Goldi: "Come on, Missi. It's obvious I'm destined for greater things than typing, fetching coffee, and taking minutes at sweaty sauna meetings."

Alice: "And I'm not?"

Goldi: "Look at it this way. Things'll be better for you when I'm Frau Hitler. I know as well as you do the scheiße that goes with being a Nazi secretary – after all, we started punching the clock here on the same day. I'll persuade Dolfi to make some changes, don't you worry about it. We'll hire a couple more girls to ease the workload. Promote *you* to head secretary. More vacation time. Maybe even get you a raise. Although that's a longshot, what with the payroll guy."

Alice: "You have it all figured out, huh?"

Goldi: "Why do you sound so upset? This is good for you, too, Missi."

Alice: "Goldi?"

Goldi: "Ja, Missi?"

Alice: "There's something I've wanted to tell you for a long time."

Goldi: "What's that?"

Alice: "My name's Alice. Not Missi. Alice."

Goldi: "But I've been calling you Missi for six –"

Alice: "For six years. And I've always hated it."

Goldi: "But I thought it was, you know, cute. Because Alice is kind of a, well, kind of a dull name. What's wrong with Missi?"

Alice: "It's demeaning. It's disrespectful. It's *sexist* – it's what a lech calls you as he stares at your busen!"

Goldi: "Well, fine!"

Alice: "You know what else? I haven't liked you very much since you started this whole lovey-dovey business with der Führer. If you keep on going with this tawdry nonsense, I don't think we can be friends anymore."

Goldi: "Is that right? Well, let me tell *you* something. I'm good for Dolfi – *damn* good. And what's good for him is good for this country. So I'm sorry, but I have to choose my country over you!"

Alice: "Bravo! How patriotic of you! I guess it's 'Deutschland über Alice,' huh?"

Goldi: "What? I don't get it."

THWAP!

No one told *me* the conversation was over! The door had flown open, and cracked my skull like a hammer on a coconut.

With one paw cradling my sore head, I tried to three-foot it out of the way of oncoming traffic. Goldi burst into the hallway, and her sharp heel found my tail.

• • •

Less than an hour later, I observed Alice in the Four Star corridor, outside the first couple's bedroom. When she was certain that no one was looking, she pulled a small object from her handbag. Then, in one quick motion, she opened the door to the room, threw the object inside, and shut the door again.

She beat a hasty retreat back to the B-B.

• • •

Later that day, I found Fräulein Braun lying in bed, reading. I hopped up to join her, and nearly fainted when I saw what she held in her hands: Goldi's blue diary.

For half an hour I remained faithfully by the side of my troubled mistress. She was eating up the secretary's words with eyes that said, *I'm going to puke!* Every few pages she muttered oaths through clenched teeth, things like "Never took *me* to no fricken jazz club!" and "So, the limp bastard can get it up for *her*, can he!"

Der Führer surprised us both when he walked in. Fräulein Braun looked up, pain and fury scrawled all over her face like a drunk musician's autograph. Hitler, heading for the dresser without so much as a peek at the bed, asked, "Coming up to the garden?"

Fräulein Braun glared at him.

"Suit yourself," he said. Turning to leave, he tucked his Schmeisser into the back of his trousers.

Someone was going to be whacked, but who? And why? Had Blondi seen Stalin again? I have a weakness for rubbernecking, and I wanted very much to witness the execution. However, when I tried to leave the room with der Führer, he proved too quick in shutting the door.

Fräulein Braun rose from the bed. This time, when the door opened, I managed to get out.

We saw Hitler marching down the corridor, towards the staircase that led to the garden. I started trotting after him, but after a moment realized that my mistress was not at my heels. When I looked over my shoulder blade, I saw her heading for the B-B.

Who to follow?

I decided on Fräulein Braun.

. . .

When two males of *Homo sapiens* prepare to engage in hand-to-hand combat, the violence, if any indeed transpires, is invariably prefaced by dilly-dallying. Among youngsters, for instance, you will hear bluster like, "Go ahead, throw the first punch!" This curious invitation is met not by a first punch, no, but by, "*I'm* not throwing the first punch! *You* throw the first punch!" There follows much waiting, with sidelong glances that practically beg for the intervention of a peacemaker. After the changing of three seasons, the assembled crowd departs in disappointment.

With full-grown men, you will see the combatants, once it has been agreed on that a physical confrontation will occur, take two steps back from their rival, as if each has detected a foul odor wafting off the other. Coats are carefully removed, and handed to a trusted bystander. Shirt-sleeves are methodically rolled up, and belts tightened. Like preprogrammed robots, the men adopt the fight poster stance of the bare-knuckled brawler, John L. Sullivan. Arms are held up and bent, naked elbows aimed at the ground. The raised left fist hovers threateningly in front. The right, tucked close to the chin, volunteers for the home guard. A pair of wide, hyper-alert eyeballs locks on its opposite. The slow circling of bodies begins. It is a perverse mating dance, these peacocks in heat who have each mistaken the other for a peahen. If a cat in need of a little diversion is lucky, there might be a blow struck in anger before next Mothering Sunday rolls around.

Not so with the female of the species, as I was so joyously reminded that day.

Goldi was alone in the lunchroom, smoking. When Fräulein Braun and I walked in, the secretary immediately tried to stub out her Lucky. I say "tried" because she had recently begun using a cigarette holder, and still had not got the hang of extinguishing cigarettes with them. In the end, she had to put the Lucky out in her coffee.[32]

"Hello, *Fräulein* Braun," Goldi said, pot-shotting my mistress's old maid status while rising to her feet.

No energy was expended on preliminaries. Without warning, Fräulein Braun lunged forward. Both arms went on the offensive. There was no "home guard" nonsense. With her left hand, my mistress grabbed Goldi's hair and pulled hard, whiplashing the secretary's head. Then Fräulein Braun used her free hand to gouge Goldi's eyeballs, *both* of the them, *at the same time!*

Now *this* – like king's pawn to e4 – was a classic opening!

Goldi, too, must be commended for eschewing all thought of self-preservation. Rather than attempt to remove the thumb and index finger imbedded deep in

---

[32] Goldi had found the cigarette holder while snooping around in one of the abandoned bunker lockers, hunting for loose change after the payroll guy turned down her request for an advance on her salary. After an inspection for teeth marks came up negative, she quickly incorporated the holder into her nicotine habit. She did this, according to her diary, in anticipation of her promotion to der Führer's wife ("Yellow fingertips would be unbecoming for a First Frau of the Third Reich. What would happen if the King of Sweden kissed my hand and then had to spit right after?"). In Goldi's defense, it really was an exquisitely designed cigarette holder, hand-made from polished honey Jade, with carvings of roses, robins, and swastikas.

either eye, she grabbed Fräulein Braun by the throat and began squeezing. By now both women were screaming, and it seemed as if neither death grip would be loosened any time soon. I kept pacing around the two, angling for the best view. Naturally, Goldi stepped on my tail again, but this time the pain was worth it!

Fräulein Braun, turning blue now, used her reach advantage to lean back and squirm out of Goldi's choke hold. She pushed the stockier woman away while her dug-in digits kept the secretary blinded. Then, in rapid fire sequence, Goldi hoofed Fräulein's Braun's shin, which saw the taller woman let go the eye gouge. With Fräulein Braun hopping on one foot and holding her bruised shin in both hands, Goldi, squinting out of one eye, threw a haymaker that caught my mistress on the chin, staggering her. With Fräulein Braun bent over and trying to regain her senses, the secretary briefly lost her focus and began showboating, raising her arms in the air and doing a little victory shuffle, with her back to her opponent. Tactical error! By the time Goldi turned around, Fräulein Braun rocked her with a right-hand upper-cut. Goldi hit the floor, and Fräulein Braun pounced on her.

Now it was a ground fight, with both women using their lefts for hair-yanking and their rights for clawing. Oh, what carnage! The secretary's forehead cut open, and my mistress had a fat lip, and both had blood streaming from their noseholes!

They were beginning to wear out, like exhausted gladiators, when the lunchroom door opened. It was der Führer, with smoking Schmeisser pistol in hand. "Verdammt!" he said, after a moment to take it all in. "This is a fine how-do-you-do!"

"And the pig," Hitler said, his eyes misty and vacant, perhaps already glimpsing some vista from his next life. Don't forget Wilbur. They all die tonight."

What kind of new madness was this? Group suicide! The slaughter of innocent pets! Popcorn as a wedding hors d'oeuvre! And who in the hell was Wilbur?

I raced to the rumpus room. I knew Blondi, who was lazier than two sloths on a Bahama holiday, spent afternoons napping there after chasing Stalins in the garden all morning. I awoke her by biting down on the end of her tail, the one proven method. Then I yelled, "Let's go!"

"Huh?" She gave her head a shake, and slowly got up on her feet. "Where are we going?"

"To buy gum!"

"I don't like gum, Tutti. I like juicy bones. I like Frau Göring's strudel. I like crayons. I like –"

"Dummkopf! Don't you get it? They want to murder us! Hitler's going to kill himself, and he wants to drag everyone down with him!"

Her mouth hung open in stunned disbelief. I moved back to avoid the inevitable puddle. Then she whispered, "Tutti, are you on catnip again?"

"*Scheiße!* You know I'm off that stuff! I've been clean for three months, twenty-eight days! I get my four month medallion on Thursday – *if* Kempka doesn't get to me first! Now, are you with me or not, Blondi? Because damn it, *I'm buying gum!*"

She grew quiet, and a grave expression fell over her. "No, Tutti," she replied at last, with a lump in her throat. I noticed that the yellow crayon was missing. "If Herr Hitler wants me to die with him, then I'll die with him."

The women extricated themselves from each other and wearily got up. "Dolfi, I'm glad you're here," Fräulein Braun said, panting. "Shoot this bitch in the neck."

"Shoot *me* in the neck? Shoot *her* in the neck!" Goldi counter-suggested.

"I'm not shooting *anybody* in the neck!" Hitler said. "I just *shot* somebody in the neck! I'm done for the day!"

Der Führer, obviously trying to escape the tense stand-off, made a move to leave the lunchroom. Fräulein Braun and Goldi had the same thought – wrestle the gun from Hitler! They pounced on him like lions on a rookie lion tamer. I ducked behind the icebox, afraid of being felled by a stray bullet. I heard them shouting and struggling like desperate old maids over a tossed wedding bouquet. Finally there was a single blast, and then an eerie calm.

I peeked out from around the icebox. All three were still standing. Goldi was looking at Hitler, and Fräulein Brain was looking at Goldi, and Hitler was looking at Fräulein Braun.

Goldi broke the silence with a small, pained cry. She collapsed to the linoleum. A stain was inching across the front of her blouse, the red overtaking the white the way the words "German Occupied" spread over maps of Europe in the early years of the war.

"Herr Gott, are you happy now?" Hitler said to his fellow survivor. "Nice fricken birthday present you got me! Gimme that gun!"

Fräulein Braun handed over the weapon. "Ja, well next time keep your big schwanz in your pants. How do I look?" She was fixing her hair. The effort did little to improve her appearance, since she was bloodier than Gene Tunney after the licking Harry Greb gave him in their first bout.

"Oh, you look *swell*, honey! Just *peachy!*" Hitler nodded at Goldi on the floor, without looking at her, and in a softer tone added, "Tell the maid to clean this up."

Hitler left the lunchroom, shaking his head in disgust.

Fräulein Braun found her purse. She retrieved her compact and nonchalantly began to reapply her makeup.

. . .

25 April, 1945.

Four days earlier, at the Elbe river, the Russkis of the 58th Guards Division met the Yanks of the US 69th Division. A Russian general shook mitts with an American general, and now Deutschland was sliced like a bread roll. All that remained was the formality of slapping a little butter on us, and then we could be properly gobbled up.

The only question was when.

. . .

29 April, 1945.

Were the Reds really unable to locate the bunker's hidden entrance, or were they toying with us? We all stole about on tippytoes because we could smell borscht boiling, and above us hear Russian voices playing Crazy Eights.

While most of the people around me grew despondent, the black cloud that had been hanging for months

over der Führer had miraculously lifted. T[...] ingly on the spur of the moment, he deci[...] knot with Fräulein Braun. He assured her [...] he was looking Death flush in the face had [...] do with him finally agreeing to marriage. Go[...] asked to be the best man, and you should [...] Bormann and "von" Ribbentrop pouting about [...]

After kissing the bride (who wore white, [...] smirking amusement of Fraus Goebbels and [...] Hitler walked over to the middle of the lunchroo[...] cleared his throat. Then he announced to all the[...] attendance his latest big idea.

Mass suicide.

"We'll make it a party game," der Führer said, try[...] to sound upbeat. "Everyone dies. Come on, it'll be fu[...]

Goebbels and his family were all for it. Borman[...] and "von" Ribbentrop played it safe. They smiled fatu[...] ously, but never actually said, "I'm in." Only the Speers voiced reservations. After consulting each other privately in hushed tones, they said they had to step out to "buy gum."

By now Hitler knew only too well what *that* meant! He glared at Speer, his longtime Minister for Armaments and Production, and, voice dripping with sarcasm, sneered, "What, you too, Brutus? Thanks for the support, *pal!*" When der Führer turned away, the Speers, looking hurt but relieved, left the bunker forever.

Then, something that chilled me to the core. Hitler put his hand on Kempka's elbow. "Round up the animals."

Kempka, whom I had always held in the highest esteem and treated not as a servant but an equal, nodded without flinching. "Gotcha, Boss. I'll get Blondi and Tutti."

I could not believe my pointy ears! Here I was, for some absurd reason trying to save the fur of the canine mental case who had been making my life so wretched, and she was rejecting my help!

She lifted a paw and placed it on my shoulder, taking care not to put too much pressure on me because, after all, she did outweigh me by about twelve to one. "Listen," she said, with tears welling in her eyes, "I can't leave. I think you know that. I've been with him for years. I don't know how many, but however many it is you multiply it by seven. And then, I don't know, you have to divide. I think by three. Or add something. I'm not exactly –"

I bopped her one on the snout.

"Ja, ja. Look, Herr Hitler's been great to me. No complaints. No sir, not one. But you, you've only been here a short while. You didn't see the glory days. You didn't have fun like I did. The fan letters I got from kids all over the world. The swell rallies and parades. The Oktoberfest where Frau Schultz broke Göring's wrist arm-wrestling him. And Chamberlain's fabulous socks! No, I'm staying."

"But you don't have to ... Wait. You got *fan* letters?"

"Thousands! But never mind that. We don't have time. You go, Tutti." She was really bawling now, and took a moment to compose herself. "Save yourself, my friend. As for me, I'm going to die with my master."

What a time for loyalty! Now I was bawling, too!

In walked Kempka, with Frau Schultz a step behind. I bolted for the door, but the cook, given her advanced years and stumpy ankles, proved curiously agile in blocking my escape. She reached down and lifted me by my loose neck fur, holding me aloft an inch from her noseholes. "Haw!"

she laughed, showering me again with her hideous dentures. "I *told* you I would make soup of you! Haw!"

I could not turn my head, but in my peripheral vision could make out Kempka patting Blondi's back. "That's a good girl," he sugared her up. "Now open wide. Uncle Erich's got a treat for you." He put out his hand, in the palm a white capsule. Blondi must have forgotten what we were just discussing, for she was so eager for her "treat" that, in scarfing it up, she bit the chauffeur's fingers!

"This one, now," Frau Schultz said.

Kempka was rubbing his bloody hand. "Stupid dog."

There was a dull thump.

"Holy Barbarossa!" Kempka said. "That stuff works fast!"

"Ja, on the dog. But this one's going to be harder," the cook said. "It knows."

I tried to squirm free. With claws out, I kicked my legs, but scratched nothing but air. Kempka stood before me with the death pill. I clenched my jaw. Frau Schultz was using one hand to pry open my mouth, and when that did not work Kempka pitched in to assist her. My brain was spinning in fear. *Clench, damn you,* I told my jaw, *clench!*

At last, the capsule was forced past my lips.

Kempka put me on the floor. I began to walk in circles. Frau Schultz chuckled. I tripped and fell. I got back up. I fell again. This time I stayed down.

The cook picked me up. She took me across the room, of course by the scruff of the neck, and dunked me into the wastebasket for two easy points. I lay motionless, with my eyes closed. I heard her dusting her hands.

Kempka said, "I thought we were supposed to bring them both to the bonfire."

"Nein," Frau Schultz said. "Der Führer changed the plan, when Fräulein Braun was in the washroom. He only wants the dog burned with him. Something about the cat's 'evil face.'"

From the bottom of the wastebasket, lying amidst coffee grinds and cigarette butts, I heard them straining to lift Blondi's dead weight. I waited a few minutes after the door had closed behind them.

Then I spit out the pill, which I had cheeked. I climbed out of the wastebasket. My neck was sore.

. . .

I spent the evening alone in the dark rumpus room. Outside the bunker Russian mortar shells erupted. Inside, floating through the ventilation ducts in the rumpus room, came the sounds of the wedding reception. Songs cranked out on the Victrola. Absurdly extravagant toasts to everyone's good health. Goebbels, Bormann, and "von" Ribbentrop, lackeys to the bitter end, complimenting der Führer on snagging such a pretty bride.

Hitler, I must say, was acting very chipper for a man laboring under the impression that both of his pets had just been murdered.

. . .

For hours there had been a great stampede through the corridor outside the rumpus room. Some folks were making their way up to the garden to kill themselves. Others were going to take their chances trying to elude capture by the Russians invaders.

Around midnight, when it had been relatively quiet for hours, the door to my prison cell opened. It was a guard I did not recognize. To go by the big half-filled sack he was lugging, he was busy looting the joint. In any case, I did not stick around to chat.

I ran down the hallway, to the exit that led to the garden. Luckily, the trap-door had been blown off by a bomb. I poked my head out of the hole like a groundhog. There were explosions in the distance, but in the garden itself all I saw was the roaring bonfire. Standing next to it, with his back to me, was a solitary figure. He was reaching into a wheel barrow filled with books. He would take one out, then pull off the cover. Then he ripped up the pages of the book and tossed them into the blaze. All this he did in a perfunctory, yet relaxed, manner.

In the flame I could see there were many bodies stacked on top of one another.

I climbed up into the garden. I had to pass the bonfire and its caretaker in order to get to the gate. When I snuck up next to him, I stopped, and looked up into his face.

He saw me, and for a moment froze in a look of shock.

Then he shrugged, and smiled that rakish smile of his. "It wasn't personal."

I turned to the gate, and walked out.